# Ma Tutt's Donut Hut

Lyn Perry

**Ma Tutt's Donut Hut**

*A Mack the Magical Cat Mystery*

Copyright © 2014 Lyndon Perry

All rights reserved.

Published by Tule Fog Press
www.tulefogpress.com

Image © RossellaApostoli/iStock
Cover Design © 2014 Jordan Dyke
jordangrfx.com

ISBN: 1500738891
ISBN-13: 978-1500738891

FOR ALL WHO NEED
A LITTLE 'MAGICAL' SPICE
IN THEIR LIVES
~*~
HERE'S TO NEW BEGINNINGS

# CONTENTS

Gratitude

# GRATITUDE

One theme of this book, as you'll discover, is gratitude.
It's always good to give thanks! And so I want to take a
moment to express my appreciation to those who've
encouraged me in the writing of this book – my wife,
my family, my beta readers, my online friends, and
my local writing group and colleagues at school.

I'm grateful to God for the gift of story and hope this
short novel serves as a testimony to the importance of
faith and thankfulness and the power of renewed life.

Of course, I'm grateful for my two cats, Izzy and Charlie,
who are great companions and together serve as
inspiration for Mack the Magical Cat.

.

And, finally, thank you for reading!
I hope you enjoy these stories.

## 'Tail' Number One
### Ma's Irresistible Doughnuts


Ma Tutt's Donut Hut sat empty on a Saturday morning. An assortment of fresh and tasty glazed, cake, and specialty doughnuts were arranged attractively in the window. Ma Tutt had gone out and approved the visual invitation herself. The sweet and enticing aroma of fried dough and sugar was present and accounted for. She'd even partaken of one or two (or maybe three) of her own creations that morning and her taste buds were still happy.

The only blemish, in her estimation, was that the log cabin-like Donut Hut wanted a bit of an exterior stain job. And an interior design makeover. A gas oven with four working stove tops would be nice along with a larger walk-in cooler. Oh, and a new fryer. Okay, so she'd bought a white elephant in her retirement. But leaving the Central Valley for small town mountain living had seemed so right at the time.

And she'd been a competent baker in her previous life. So when opportunity knocked....

At least the shop had come with a mature tabby, a generic gray Mackerel, who was friendly enough, if a bit demanding. Uncertain as to what to make of him that first month, she'd allowed 'Mack' to follow her around as she took those few weeks to set up shop. He eventually wormed his way into her heart with his guttural conversations and was now her steadfast companion and confidant.

Her grand opening on the first of May was successful enough, but now, a month later, business was already lagging. And at the start of tourist season! Her mountain cabin bakery was at the north end of town, a small community called Sugar Pine Station, nestled in the lower steeps of the Sierra Nevadas. Weekend tourists on their way to Yosemite or the mighty Redwoods usually found a reason to stop for a bite to eat and take a break from the winding roads. But this morning, nary a customer had entered her establishment, not even for a cup of her delicious coffee.

"I'm a failure, Mack," she murmured.

Dolores Tutt—Ma Tutt to her adopted community and Dolly to her friends and family who still lived just south of Fresno—sighed and huffed a stray strand of graying hair out of her face. She was almost retirement age, probably could have made it on her savings, but the thought of fulfilling a life-long dream of owning her own place was just too much of a temptation. Now she was thinking she should have just said no when the realtor showed her the empty building a few months back. No to pipe dreams and half hopes.

Coming out from behind the counter, she gazed through the front window at the new Creamy Pie and scowled as her resolve strengthened. Darned franchises were ruining quaint towns like hers. Like hers? She laughed quietly. Even as a new resident of Sugar Pine Station, she'd quickly developed a fierce loyalty to this scenic village. She'd made some good friends upon her arrival, and she already had a few regular customers, but not nearly enough to sustain the bakery for the long haul. She and Mack had to do something.

Nodding at the brisk business taking place across the street, she muttered to the tabby, "We deserve something better than some sterile, cookie-cutter outfit that lacks the picturesque charm of, say, the Hut!" Mack swished his tail and gave her a sidelong glance that looked to her quite condescending. "Okay, I deserve better. At least I don't deserve to starve!" The cat let out a purr and insisted on a backrub. Dolly complied and chuckled gently as she turned her back on the competition and headed for the kitchen.

Cleaning was her default mode when fighting off any kind of disquiet. So taking a towel and running it under the faucet, she started in, wiping down every available surface of the bakery. She didn't worry whether someone might accidently venture into the store, she'd hear the tinkling of bells attached to the front door. That and Mack would usually announce a customer some way or another, typically with a loud series of meows. As she worked, the cat jumped from counter top to prep table, pointing out areas that needed attention.

"It's almost as if you understand what's going on here, kitty. Thanks for your help."

When the obvious spots were sparkling, and there were still no prospects for her delicious delights, she tossed her towel in the wash sink and faced a large wooden cabinet that reigned like Pharaoh along the back wall of the kitchen. It was a ramshackle imitation antique of a thing that had come with the Hut—chockfull of old cookbooks and random stashes of recipe cards—and something she hadn't had time to fully inspect or organize since opening a few weeks back.

She looked over the disaster and sighed. She needed backroom counter space and this monstrosity not only took up too much room, it was simply an eyesore. It probably should have been hauled out when she bought the place but she'd given up that idea after grabbing at it in a feeble attempt to move it. It wasn't going anywhere any time soon. So she'd left it alone. At least it was pushed in the corner and somewhat out of the way. All it could stand at this point was a good cleaning.

Ma Tutt clapped her hands together. The time had finally come to tackle it.

"Are you going to help me or just sit there and supervise?"

Mack yawned.

"Thought as much. So first thing we ought to do, excuse me, *I* ought to do, is take out all the books and such. Get a clear picture of what we've got. Who knows? Could be a hidden treasure in this thing!"

The tabby mewed politely.

"Then it's settled."

Dolly found a couple of empty boxes and started transferring the contents of the cabinet into them. It turned out that the hutch yielded not too horribly many books, and she completed her task by the third cardboard carton. She then collected all the loose papers, index cards, and food-related magazine clippings. A fourth container was needed for that and when it was filled, she wiped her hands like Pilate at the trial of Jesus.

Mack jumped onto the cabinet and explored the empty shelves. He pawed at a shut drawer. "I think that's all for today, Mack. That one's empty, see?"

She pulled open the drawer and the tabby crawled in, offering a guttural commentary that only cats can give.

"Hey, get out of there, you'll get stuck." She opened the drawer all the way and saw Mack pawing at a corner of a recipe card wedged in the back. "Okay, smarty pants. There's one left. Here, let me grab it." She first pried the cat loose then tried sliding the card out from between the wooden slats. Mack meowed. "Hello, it's harder than it looks!"

Right as she was about to achieve victory, the front door gave out a jingle. Surprised, Dolly gave one final tug and pulled the card free, minus a small corner. She glanced at it quickly, noting the faded handwriting along with the heading: *Irresistible Doughnuts*. Intriguing. But later! She placed it back in the drawer, tucked a few errant strands of hair into her hairnet, and hurried to the front of the store.

"Good morning!" she called out in greeting. A trim man, probably in his early thirties wearing the standard blue work shirt of a technician with a schedule to keep, indicated the clock above the kitchen's entrance. Ma Tutt followed his gaze—*one o'clock!*—and then turned back with a slight grimace. "Good afternoon then. Can I interest you in a fresh glazed doughnut? A specialty cupcake? An apple turnover?"

"Sorry, just need you to sign here." He handed a clipboard across the counter. "There at the bottom."

"What's this?" She frowned as she skimmed the piece of paper. She looked up and noticed his name emblazoned on the shirt right above the pocket. Donovan Huckly. Under it, in italic script, was the tag line, *Utility Compliance*.

"Shut off notice. Electricity. You have a week to pay in full or the utility company pulls the plug, so to speak."

"Five thousand and forty-seven dollars?" Ma Tutt wasn't one to sputter, at least not as a matter of course, but, "This…this…this can't be! I just opened the shop a month ago. This must be the previous owner's bill." A wave of relief washed over her. "Oh, see here? It has her name at the top, Martía Cooper."

Donovan Huckly gave the clipboard a cursory glance without taking it. "Same address, I'm afraid. And the bill's past due. You can always call the company, but I still need your signature."

"And if I refuse?" Dolly straightened her back.

"Same result. I just make a note that you were notified. You have a week to pay or we shut off the juice."

Ma Tutt let the clipboard clatter to the countertop and wiped her suddenly sweaty palms on her apron.

"Don't shoot the messenger, ma'am." He picked up the paperwork, scribbled a few sentences at the bottom, and turned to leave. He stopped when he saw the tray of chocolate covered cake doughnuts. "Oh, hey, since it's late in the day, are those half off yet?" He smiled hopefully.

Some gall! But it was a sale, and could be her only one that day. Swallowing her pride, she forced a smile and said, "How about two for one?"

"Deal." The young man pulled some loose change from his pocket, received a bag with a pair of chocolate creations in exchange, and left.

Ma Tutt collapsed into the chair behind the cash register. It was almost one-thirty and the Donut Hut had seventy-five cents in the till. Whee.

Mack sauntered up and rubbed the full length of his body against her leg. Past time for a snack. She gave in and poured some dry food in his dish.

"You're irresistible, and don't you know it," she said to her friend as she put away the food. "Speaking of which." Dolly returned to the not-so-antique hutch and opened the right hand drawer.

She pulled out the recipe card and examined it, both front and back. *Irresistible Doughnuts.* The handwriting was old fashioned and was fading a bit, but it seemed in order. She had enough experience baking to know this recipe was industrial size; she could do math, though, and was already considering cutting it in half, or maybe down to a quarter batch.

Looking closely at the list of ingredients, she realized the torn corner had obscured a final spice. Kicking herself for ripping the card, she pulled the drawer out as far as it could go and felt around for the remaining scrap. She couldn't find it.

Dolly scratched the back of Mack's ears. "Well, we can always improvise. Let's try it tomorrow, shall we?"

The gray tabby offered what she thought was another condescending look. "Well, I'm going to whether you help me or not."

The next morning, bright and early—well, it wasn't bright yet!—Dolly unlocked the Donut Hut and made her way to the kitchen, leaving the front lights off. She'd debated whether or not to open on

Sundays, and she still had an hour or so to consider it before anyone in their right mind would want breakfast. While blue laws were passé, this was still Small Town America after all. She knew Creamy Pie would light up in an hour, with its glaring neon, so maybe she would go ahead and open; the Hut could be a quiet alternative to the loud colors.

Too quiet!

Where was Mack? He'd insisted on staying in the store when she tried to take him home with her after their first meeting. Normally, he'd greet her at the door and cheer her on as she made her way to the bin of cat food. This morning, when she turned on the kitchen lights, he was on the counter sitting patiently, serving as a bookend to a line of ceramic containers, jars of ingredients, and a slew of utensils, measuring cups, and mixing bowls.

Dolly's eyes grew wide. "What's this?" She blinked and pinched the bridge of her nose, hoping to shake off the vision. When she squinted through her fingers and saw that nothing had changed, she dropped her hands and stared, mouth agape. "Did I set all this out last night?" *Of course, must have.* She tried to remember how old she was. Sixty next month. Not that old.

Mack meowed and dipped his nose to the counter. Dolly went to him, gave him a pat and noticed an index card at his feet. She pulled it out from under his paw and read it. She gulped.

After a nervous chuckle, she said, "So you're

going to help me after all?"

The cat stood and sidled up for a back scratch. She complied and stood there contemplating the items spread out before her. She looked at the recipe for those Irresistible Doughnuts and, satisfied that most everything she'd need was on the counter already, pinned it to the corkboard. Puffing out a pent up breath, and with a curious glance at Mack, Dolly found her apron. Seeing how everything was ready, there was nothing left to do but go ahead and mix up a batch, right? Maybe this was a sign. A freakin', heart-stopping, nervous-breakdown kind of sign, but one she simply couldn't slough off.

Seemingly satisfied that his job was done, Mack jumped from the counter and wandered off. Dolly shook her head and dove in. She'd start with a quarter batch and evaluate the results when done. Ah, the art of baking. Her creative side kept telling her to tweak the recipe as she progressed, but she couldn't shake the feeling that she'd be better served following the details exactly.

Except when she came to the last spice. The card was torn, and 'a pinch of...*something*' was left to the imagination. She surveyed the selection of jars and containers that Mack—no, it had to have been her the night before—had arranged on the counter. One small tin remained untouched. She picked it up and examined it. *Iseult*. She'd never heard of it. She opened it. Smelled it. Tasted it. It was a bit salty....

She wrinkled her nose and was about to put it

down when she thought, why not? She took a pinch and tossed it in the batter. The deep fat fryer was ready and she soon had about three dozen fresh doughnuts in, out, and cooling on the rack. They were rather plain looking. Nothing to distinguish them from her regular cake doughnuts and she considered sprinkling them with cinnamon sugar. Half of them, she decided, she would. Tasting one she'd lightly coated, she nodded and smiled.

Not bad. Not bad at all.

At 5:15, Ma Tutt flipped on all the lights, unlocked the front door, and declared her store open for business. She beat Creamy Pie to the punch by fifteen minutes, though she could see a few teenagers drag themselves around inside getting ready for the day. A car pulled into the parking lot across the street and she grumbled under her breath. Let the doughnut wars begin. She propped the door open so the aroma of fresh baked goods could work its magic.

When a man walked by, slowly, dressed for early morning mass, she greeted him on the sidewalk with a sample tray of her daybreak creations. "Free doughnut?"

He blinked. "Um, sure. I was actually heading across the way, but couldn't help but smell your...offerings." He plucked a regular 'Irresistible' from the tray and, after a bite, nodded in satisfaction. "Mmm. Very moist. Is that fresh coffee brewing?"

Ma Tutt led him inside and poured him a full cup. He sat at the counter and lost himself in his newfound ambrosia. A car pulled up in front of the Hut and, engine still running, another man popped in. "Didn't know this place had re-opened. Saw it when I pulled in over there." He thumbed the competition. "Something told me I just had to drop in. What are you serving?"

"A variety of day-olds at half price; but fresh this morning, a new recipe." No mention of free this time. She knew a thing or two about supply and demand.

"It's verra good," the man at the counter said, his mouth full. "I'll have another." He pulled out a dollar bill and handed it over.

"Two to go, no cinnamon," said the man with the running engine, "and a coffee, two creams."

"Coming right up."

When she finished those orders, two women in running gear slipped in as the drive-up guy left. They exchanged embarrassed looks. "Uh, time to refuel," said one. "Yeah," agreed the other and pointed. "Whatever he's having."

"They're verra good," Mr. Counter-man said again. "I'll have another."

Ma Tutt raised an eyebrow, but wasn't one to judge. She served her customers and the steady trickle of newcomers that followed suit over the next few hours. Mr. Drive-up guy even came back, this time with his family. They camped themselves in a corner booth and, after gobbling down two pastries each, took a dozen home when they left. She was soon down to her last Irresistible Doughnut, one brushed with cinnamon, along with one customer, Mr. Counter-man.

"I guess I'll have that one too. I already missed church, so what's the harm in one more?"

*Other than clogged arteries and an early heart attack?* But Ma Tutt served it up just the same and watched, mesmerized, as the man put it to his lips. One bite, however, and the spell was broken. The church-dressed counter-man put the remaining doughnut back on his plate and groaned.

"*Ooof.* That about does it for me. What time do you open tomorrow?"

"Well...I..." Ma Tutt calculated how long it would take for her to make a half batch the next morning. "Five o'clock sharp," she said at last. That would beat Creamy Pie by thirty minutes.

"I'll be here." The man rose slowly from the swivel stool and stumbled out the door, holding his belly.

"Well, I swear!" she muttered to herself.

Mack mewed a response.

"And where have you been hiding all morning?"

This time the gray tabby let out a plaintive *mrrow* and jumped up on the counter. Lunch time. Dolly looked at the clock on the wall, and indeed, it was already past noon. She glanced at the empty display racks. Just a few stray turnovers remained. "Unbelievable! I guess we better close up shop, Mack."

Before she could move from behind the cash

13

register, however, one more person jingled through the front door. She scowled at him. "You again?"

"I'm not here about the electricity," he said, his hands up in surrender. The name on his work shirt was still Donovan Huckly, but he wore a different colored work shirt than the day before. Forest Green this time.

"Okay, then, Mr. Huckly. What can I do for you? We're almost sold out."

"I'm not here for a doughnut either."

Not in the mood for guessing games, Dolly let out an exasperated sigh. "Then what are you here for?"

The young man produced another clipboard, as if he kept a supply hidden somewhere behind his back. "On Sundays, I work part time for Animal Control; we're a part of the county's Health Department. When I was in yesterday, I noticed your cat." He nodded at Mack, who was giving himself a bath on the glass countertop. "Can't have pets in a food service business. I'm afraid I'm going to have to remove him from the premises."

"You're gonna have to do what?"

"I think you heard me, ma'am."

The two met each other's glares like gunslingers on a Saturday Western television show.

"Over my dead body." If she could pistol whip him, she would.

"Now, let's not be so melodramatic."

Dolly steeled herself for a showdown while Mack

looked on, dispassionate.

After a few moments of ominous silence, Donovan broke the tension, beads of sweat betraying his calm demeanor. "I tell you what. I'll write up a warning this time. But I'm going to drop in tomorrow. And if that cat is inside this store, I'll be forced to…to deal with it." He punctuated his threat with a finger poke to the air.

Before she could respond, the full time meter reader/part time animal control fanatic spun on his heel and made for the door. He stopped abruptly and turned his head. "Are those turnovers free yet?"

"Out!"

And out he went, slamming the door behind him which conveniently flipped the sign from Open to Closed. The emotion of the day caught up with her and Dolly stumbled into the chair behind the register. Mack sprang to her lap and nuzzled up under her chin, communicating everything would be all right.

"You think so?" She sighed and rubbed her temples. "I hope you're right, dear kitty. I truly hope so."

When Mack was done with his consoling, he jumped down, signaling it was time to lock the front door and tidy up. She heaved her weary body out of the chair and went about her closing routine. Taking the money from the register, she said, "I'll count this at home. I'll be back early tomorrow and we can start it all over again." The cat meowed in agreement.

Lights off, and with a final scan and nod, Dolly

went through the kitchen and let herself out the back door, leaving Mack to his own devices.

At 3:30 the next morning, Ma Tutt was back, yawning. She flipped on some lights and Mack greeted her with his usual starvation call. "A bit early for breakfast, isn't it?" After absentmindedly pouring a few bits of kibble into his dish, she shuffled to the kitchen. She was surprised that she wasn't surprised to see the counter lined up with all the ingredients to make another batch of Irresistible Doughnuts.

So she got right to work, mixing up a half portion of the recipe this time. Before sprinkling in a double pinch of *Iseult* spice, the tabby jumped on the counter and pawed the card still tacked to the corkboard. "That's right, Mack. We're making more. Good kitty." Mack let out a low growl. "Now, now. No need to be rude." She tried to pet him with her free hand. He yowled again and took a swipe at her. "Mister!" Ignoring him, she tossed in the unusual ingredient. Then pinched in another for good measure.

Time was slipping away and she bustled about preparing trays of scones and other pastries to meet the day's demands. At least she hoped there would be a demand. Her spirits lifted when the Donut Hut soon filled with the familiar and enticing aroma of fresh baked goods. At 4:45 she heard banging at the front of the store.

"What in the world?" Ma Tutt made her way

from the kitchen and gaped. She hit the lights—a dozen or more people were standing outside. The man who missed church was pounding on the plate glass window. "One moment! We'll open soon!" *Oh, my.* She hurried to shelve the last of the doughnuts, foregoing any sprinkles or decorations. If people were that hungry, they could just eat them plain this morning.

"Remind me to hire some help this week, Mack." But the tabby had made himself scarce. "Just as well," she muttered, remembering Mr. Donovan Cat-hater. Another round of banging on the window had her looking at the clock—4:55!—and scurrying to greet the customers. She flipped the sign to Open and unlocked the door. The people poured in.

For the next three hours she couldn't find thirty seconds to relax. People came and went, came back, brought friends; parked themselves at the counter, in booths, at tables; ordered seconds, thirds, fourths; helped themselves to coffee, made more coffee; left money, left tips, left their senses.

Just when she was about to bring out the last tray of goodies, the jingling bells announced another customer. With an automatic, "Welcome to Ma Tutt's Donut Hut," she looked up and saw Huckly enter the store. She groaned and quickly glanced about for Mack.

Clipboard in hand, he said, "Just a friendly reminder that your electricity will be cut…." The evil meter reader looked around at all the people, inhaled deeply, smiled, and snagged a barstool next to the man who'd missed church. "I'll have what he's having."

"It's verra good."

Ma charged him double.

Soon the shelves were empty. It was just past ten o'clock. She wondered how to break the news; she normally closed the bakery by 1 p.m.

"Sorry, friends, but I'm afraid we're sold out. I want to thank you all, of course, but it's time to, well, close up shop for the day."

*Aws* and *Ohs* and *Nos* and one *Dagnabbit* met her announcement. But after a few grumblings and inquiries as to what time the Hut would be open in the morning, the crowd eventually left, leaving her with a mess worthy of FEMA intervention. Mack made his appearance at last and surveyed the damage with a meow that sounded a whole lot like 'I told you so.'

"You told me what, silly cat? That I should have made more? How was I to know after such a dismal few weeks? Now I'm wondering if I've taken on a bit more than I can chew." Mack offered a little chirrup. "So to speak." Grabbing a wet hand cloth, she started wiping down tables and clearing dirty dishes. She headed back to the dishwasher and was already planning the next day's selections; a full batch of Irresistible Doughnuts was an obvious menu choice. They'd made good on the name, that was for certain. As she considered that, something tugged at the back of her mind about the recipe.

Before she could pinpoint what was bothering her, a crash of breaking glass caused her to jump and cry out. She rushed through the doorway separating the kitchen from the dining area and screamed. There was Mr. Counter-man, leading a pack of desperate looking people as they clawed their way through the front window. A glassy-eyed Donovan was close behind, along with the two runner women from Sunday morning. They took their places around the room and, without even a by-your-leave, started licking the crumbs from the tables.

Dolly watched, agog.

Sugar packets were next. Torn open and emptied into eager mouths. An eerie absence of conversation amplified the clattering of silverware and clacking of dishes as the crowd reached for anything edible. Packets of honey and jelly were quickly consumed. Salt and pepper dispensers were opened and the contents downed like shots of whisky. People were on the floor, under the tables, scraping old gum from hidden places. The only mission that mattered was the stuffing of mouths.

Dirty napkins didn't have a chance. Nor the clean ones; the metal containers eagerly released their contents. Dolly stepped aside, alarmed, when a woman sprinted past her and brought back the trash can, dumping its contents on the floor. Like children under a broken piñata, people scrambled for goodies. Donovan found the stash of coffee and threw foil pouches over his shoulder, sharing his bounty. Into the kitchen more people ran and the search was on. Flour flew. Baking soda sailed by. Sugar and spice and everything nice disappeared before Dolly's eyes.

Helpless and unable to stop the madness, she found herself backed against the wooden hutch with Mack who, ping-pong style, took in every move of the frenetic mob. The place was in shambles. When it looked like everything edible was just about gone, the small crowd came to a jolting stop. Blank-eyed and drooling, Dolly's new customers, indeed, her new neighbors and friends, turned as one to face her.

Mr. Counter-man said, breathlessly, "You look verra good."

Dolly whimpered. Leaning against the dilapidated cabinet, she reached blindly behind her for anything that might serve as a defense of some sort. Past the mob were her kitchen knives, but there was no hope of reaching them. She might be able to make a dash for the back door before the mob closed in. For now they stood there, waiting.

Mack pawed at a drawer.

"Not now, Mack. This is serious."

*Mrrar. Mrrar, mrr, mrrrrr.* He tapped the drawer a few more times.

Dolly pulled it open in frustration and a small bottle of cinnamon rolled to the front. Something clicked in her mind as she pulled it out and stared at it.

The sight of more food brought the crowd out of their trance. They shambled forward, eyes transfixed on the spice. Without much more than a wish and a prayer, she twisted off the cap and broadcast the bottle's ingredients over the crowd like a fairy with pixie dust. She even blew out any remaining spice from the clear colored jar, accidently inhaling it when done. A fit of coughing had her bent over, desperate for breath.

With a few more hacking coughs, she finally straightened up and wiped her tearing eyes. It took her a moment to realize the mob was no longer advancing. In fact, they were starting to disperse, wandering back to the front of the diner, confused looks playing across their faces.

People began leaving with awkward shrugs and muttered apologies. Few made eye contact. Some were still clearly muddled. They stepped over broken dishes, shuffled through trash, grabbed their belongings, and left.

No less confused, but now quite miffed, Ma Tutt called out as the last one escaped. "Didn't I tell you we were all sold out?"

Later that night, after the window had been boarded up and the interior of Ma Tutt's Donut Hut had been swept back to as much order as it could manage under the circumstances, Mack came purring up to Dolly's ankles.

"You've been a great help, dear kitty." She reached down and picked him up. "Something tells me you knew what was going to happen all along."

*Mrrow.*

"Then why didn't you say anything? *Iseult!* Who ever heard of such a spice? I'll have to google it." The gray tabby nudged her chin and purred all the more. "And next time I make a quarter batch of those doughnuts, you'll have to show me what a quarter *pinch* looks like."

Mack nuzzled close and Dolly laughed. "But for now, I think I need a vacation."

## 'Tail' Number Two
## Memory Cake

It took a few weeks, but Ma Tutt's Donut Hut was back in business. And by now she had a steady flow of customers—whether out of guilt for their role in the disaster or out of a genuine desire for her baked goods, Dolly didn't care. She was just happy her insurance company had cut her a check without too much of a hassle. There was some question as to whether the disaster was actually an Act of God, but in the end they paid up and the contractors she hired refurbished the store in record time.

As she came through the back door, Mack greeted her with his usual arsenal of scoldings and promptings. Breakfast was any time after midnight, in his opinion, and four in the morning was none too early to feast on kibble. Ma Tutt turned on the lights and filled his bowl half way.

"More later, Mr. Tubby Tummy. You've got to

start watching your weight."

Mack responded with a surly *mrrow*.

Dolores Tutt was a matronly woman who, like Mack, had a taste for delectable treats. She'd decided that her early retirement years could best be enjoyed in her own pastry shop. With no children of her own, she considered herself an extra mom to her many nieces and nephews. An indulgent mamma, her siblings called her. So the name of Ma Tutt's Donut Hut, though a bit silly to her friends and family back in Fresno, seemed just right for her personality and her adopted mountain community of Sugar Pine Station.

She surveyed the refurbished bakery and smiled. The memory of the odd catastrophe with the *Irresistible Doughnuts* was slowly receding as she faced the future. Most of the patrons who had participated in the ransacking—albeit under the influence of some kind of extreme hypnosis or, a few claimed, a magical spell—returned to help clean up and start the process of rejuvenation, for which she was quite grateful.

The cozy café now boasted a much improved interior, new furnishings, and a host of modern appliances. The kitchen, almost perfect except for the presence of an ugly corner cabinet too heavy to move, complemented the service area, which was just right for socializing. There were now two corner booths for large families and gatherings of friends; near the new plate glass window were some comfy chairs suitable for relaxed conversations, along with some end tables for newspapers and magazines; and in the central dining area were now three two-tops and two four-tops that could be arranged in any number of combinations for parties large or small. And of course, throw in Ma's delicious pastries to top it all off and the place was better than new.

With a nod of satisfaction, Dolly Tutt hopped to it, and after an hour or so of flurry and preparation she was ready for the Monday morning rush.

One of the first to jingle the front door open was a new regular customer, Father Emilio Aguilera, an elderly priest who faithfully served the parish of St. Anne's Catholic Church. He entered the bakery to the tinkling of chimes and with a twinkle in his eye. Mack ran to greet him and the aging man of God bent down and whispered a hello.

"Good morning, Father," greeted Dolly, still somewhat surprised at the feline's reception of her new best customer. Mack seemed to have bonded with the priest from the first day he dropped in a few weeks back. Normally the tabby was quite standoffish and didn't mix well with others—especially the young man from Animal Control, Donovan Huckly. Fortunately, Mack now disappeared whenever Mr. Huckly dropped in, so the part-time health inspector no longer bothered her about 'getting rid of that cat.' She guessed it was a matter of don't ask, don't tell, which was fine with her.

"A good morning indeed, Ma! I see you're

expecting a busy day." He indicated the full shelves of goodies. "Smells delicious as usual." Fresh doughnuts and the aroma of coffee have a certain appeal to people of all ages, it seems.

"I certainly hope so. Business has definitely picked up these past few weeks. Getting more tourists, too." She shot her eyes across the street, leaned over the counter, and lowered her voice conspiratorially. "I think the Hut's beating the competition."

The Hut, as it was now mostly known around their small mountain community of about fifteen hundred people, was a quaint log cabin-like structure. It had become a rather popular gossip stop in the daily routine for many of the locals. Dolly noted with much satisfaction that there were fewer and fewer cars at the Creamy Pie franchise across the street. Even the day trippers to the Sequoias, who seemingly preferred fast food to authentic fare, were becoming frequent customers. Especially since she put a sign in her window, "Now Serving Cappuccinos!"

Straightening up, she asked, "Can I offer you your usual bear claw with two pats of butter?" Father Aguilera said yes and Dolly handed him his plate. "Regular and decaf coffee are now self-serve and on your honor. Just put what you wish in the jar next to the coffee urns. If you want an espresso or latte, it'll take but a few minutes."

"No, no. I'll help myself to some coffee in a moment. You've done an amazing job turning this place around. And yes, I do believe the Hut is winning the doughnut wars." He chuckled and shuffled off to his favorite chair by the window where Mack was waiting for him patiently. A steaming cup of coffee perched on an end table was waiting for the priest as well.

Dolly blinked her eyes and choked out, "Ah…thank you. Yes, it's been quite…er, miraculous. If you'll pardon the expression." She blinked again and decided to ignore the coffee mug next to Mack.

Instead she turned and gazed across the way at the Creamy Pie and allowed herself a satisfied smile. Not that she wished her competition ill will but it was nice to know that her efforts were being rewarded. Well, her efforts along with a little help from Mack and that special spice he'd found.

*Iseult!*

She'd finally looked it up and the word was actually a name, a tragic reference to a princess who fell in love with a handsome knight named Tristan after they shared a sip of love potion…which then led to all kinds of disastrous results.

Well, that made sense. The spice must have been some kind of love potion ingredient for those unique doughnuts she'd made and, boy, did it end in disaster. That is, until, with Mack's uncanny prompting, she figured out the proper ratios. After an occasional use of the magical spice brought in a steady flow of customers, she decided to stash it away for a rainy day.

Magical. Hmm. Mack certainly was special…but magical? She glanced again at the cup of coffee *someone* had served the priest just moments before. Oh, phooey. Maybe she'd set it there out of habit in anticipation of his arrival. He was now a fixture of the place. Just like Mack. Ah, another mystery…she wondered how long they'd actually known each other.

Before she could inquire as to their relationship, the gray mackerel hissed and darted off the priest's lap and into the kitchen. She gathered up her apron and said, "Well, I never…"

A moment later, the front door opened to another jingle and in walked Donovan Huckly. He had a frown on his face and was looking suspiciously at the swinging door that separated the kitchen from the dining area.

"I don't have to remind you that pets are not allowed in buildings dedicated to food service." Huckly had a way of officializing even the most obvious of statements.

*Don't ask, don't tell.* Dolly declined to comment.

"At any rate, I'm not here as an Animal Control Officer today. So nothing to worry about. For now."

Dolly wasn't necessarily worried, but she was a bit wary of the city official. He'd been appointed by Mayor Tompkins as the small town's all-purpose civic administrator. Depending on the color of the shirt he wore, residents could tell in what capacity he was acting. He took his various jobs very seriously.

Too seriously.

Today, however, he sported from top to bottom a ridiculous Ranger Rick outfit—a floppy hat suitable for the Australian outback; a khaki, short-sleeved shirt with two breast pockets; some knee-length hiking shorts held in place with an old Cub Scout belt; and finally, a pair of gray woolen socks to go with his well-worn hiking boots. Oh, and he was holding his ever present clipboard. Dolly hated that clipboard.

"I see you're going hiking this morning," Ma acknowledged. "Came in for a pastry to start your day?"

"Only if you're running a half-off special on those cinnamon buns?" Huckly asked hopefully. Ma folded her arms like a guard at Fort Knox. "Oh, well. Then I'll grab a cup of coffee. I heard you can pay what you want, right?" Donovan headed over to the coffee station and filled himself a large cup of dark roast. He plopped a quarter in the jar.

Dolly heard the priest chuckle.

So did the wannabe Eagle Scout. "Oh, hello Father." He shuffled his feet.

"Good morning, Donovan. Missed you at mass yesterday."

"Oh, yeah, well, you see...I was busy getting ready for today's hike. Wanted to explore up the mountain a bit. Up here behind the Hut." He stole a glance at Dolly who was pretending not to listen. "Uh, if that's all right with you, Ma..." He trailed off, still shifting from one foot to the other.

She looked up and thought about it for a moment. She did in fact own a few hundred yards of mountainside behind her business before the land became public property. "Well, seein' as how you were able to resolve that electric bill before we reopened, I suppose I won't mind you trekking up the hill a bit behind the Hut."

The five thousand dollar past due notice Huckly had presented her a month before had almost given Ma a heart attack. But evidently, he'd finally determined that the previous owner was responsible and dropped the matter once and for all.

"Ah, yeah, that's right." Donovan seemed to gain a bit of confidence with Dolly's acquiescence. "And actually, Father Aguilera helped me see the light, as it were, about that overdue notice."

That was odd. What did the priest have to do with utility bills? But then, Dolly wasn't one to question the Fates. She'd had a run of good luck and that's all that mattered. Mack hadn't been carted off to the pound, the electric bill was taken care of, the Hut was back in business, and better than before. Life was good. What harm could come from allowing the annoying Mr. Huckly access to the hillside in her backyard? Just a mountain slope of boulders, pine, and scrub. Have at it.

"Enjoy your hike, then," she said, dismissing the young man. He took the opportunity to escape with his steaming cup of coffee.

"I think you'll have to put up a sign by the

dispensers: 'Minimum Donation, $1.00'," Father Aguilera said, still shaking his head.

"I think you're right!"

The door opened and the steady flow of morning customers began, cutting off Ma's bubbling curiosity about the priest's curious connections with Mack and now Donovan. She soon forgot whatever questions she'd filed away for later as she spent the next few hours keeping up with the surge of business. By the time lunch time rolled around, she was sold out. Life was good. She flipped the sign from Open to Closed and locked the door.

Mack returned to help clean up. Well, he didn't actually do any of the cleanup himself, though if he did have any magical powers that could assist in the process, Dolly wouldn't have complained. No, he simply ran from spot to spot, pointing out areas that needed attention. Dirty dishes to put away, a table to wipe down, some napkins to pick up off the floor. He was as good a supervisor as Dolly had ever known.

As she was about to hit the lights, a knock at the window grabbed her attention. It was Father Aguilera.

"Sorry to bother you," the priest began once Dolly let him inside, "but I seemed to have misplaced an index card. I wonder if I left it on the table near where I sat this morning."

"Let's take a look."

Together they inspected the area where the priest usually camped out on weekday mornings. He was only there for thirty minutes or so, though Dolly told him he could stay as long as he wanted. He once teased back that he didn't want to be mistaken for an Occupy participant, but thanked her all the same.

"Truth is, I had something that I thought you might find interesting. I brought a recipe card with me this morning, but didn't have a chance to show it to you before the Hut got busy."

"That, and Mr. Huckly can be quite an inter-ruption regardless of how busy it is," Dolly noted.

"Very true."

Mack, never far behind, jumped into the padded chair and pawed at the seat cushion. He was purring triumphantly. Dolly picked him up, handed him to the priest, and pulled back the cushion. The index card had slipped down between it and the arm rest. Missing card found.

"You should go into business, dear kitty," Dolly said as she scratched his head. "Private Investigator Mack, specializing in finding lost items."

The cat flashed her a withering look that told her what he thought of that idea.

Father Aguilera set the feline down and took the card from Dolly. He pointed at the label: *Memory Cake*. The title alone was intriguing, but Ma Tutt immediately wondered at the scrawling script of the recipe card. It looked to be the same handwriting as many of the ones she'd found in the old wooden cabinet that loomed large in the kitchen.

"I have all the ingredients at home," the priest explained, unaware of Dolly's fascination, "except for one spice. It's something I've not heard of and I'm wondering if you might have it. And if so, could I borrow it?"

"Why, you certainly may, if I happen to have it. There are a few odd bottles in an old wooden cabinet in the kitchen. I think the previous owner must have left them along with a number of recipe cards...just like this one."

The priest handed her the yellowed card. "Yes, Martía and Rohan left quite suddenly last year. She'd given me a number of cards as well. Recipes she told me to try, but I do very little baking." He shook his head sadly.

"Martía...Cooper? Was that her name? I remember seeing her listed as the previous owner when Mr. Huckly came in with the overdue electric bill." Dolly cringed. No wonder they'd left so suddenly. Still, they should have paid the five thousand dollars if they owed it. She harrumphed in quiet condemnation.

"They didn't leave because of the bills," Father Aguilera said, prompting Dolly to flush with embarrassment. She hadn't meant for her suspicions to be so transparent. "The truth of the matter is that Rohan and Martía are Gypsies and sometimes they just move on without explanation."

"Gypsies?" Dolly allowed her judgmental nature to surface once more. "Aren't they *known* for sneaking off in the middle of the night?"

"I suppose some are, but the Coopers are a quite

wonderful couple. They were faithful worshipers at St. Anne's and before she left Martía gave me enough money to cover any outstanding bills they'd incurred. When I heard Donovan was threatening you with a shut-off notice, I spoke with him and quietly took care of it." Dolly nodded, relieved at the news. "Martía also instructed me to put the building up for sale if they hadn't returned by Christmas. So in January I contacted a realtor on their behalf. Six months later, here you are."

Ma Tutt was somewhat familiar with the history of the building. Before she bought the place, her realtor had run through the highlights. The log cabin was built in 1938, originally opened as a bait and tackle shop, then became a general store and served the community and vacationers in that capacity off and on for fifty-some odd years until someone (the Coopers, evidently) turned it into a cozy diner and baked goods store. It had never hosted a tremendously successful business, but Dolly hoped the Hut would prove to be the exception.

"Interesting." Gypsies, eh? She decided to withhold further judgment…for now. "Well, I'm certainly glad Mrs. Cooper left behind a few spices and recipe cards, believe you me. Let's see if we can find what you're looking for, Father." She studied the list of ingredients. "Hmm, yes. Okay, these are all fine. Looks like it'll make a delicious spice cake. But you're right, along with the nutmeg, there's a call for a quarter teaspoon of *Memoria*. Pretty easy to see how the cake got its name, but to be honest, I've never heard of it."

Together they made their way into the kitchen and stood in front of the hutch like suppliants before their king. Mack was back in his supervisory role. He hopped up on the counter and pawed at the left cupboard door.

"Yes, Mack, that's where I keep the jars I don't know what to do with."

The priest laughed quietly. "I think *he* thinks he knows what to do with them."

"Oh, if you only knew," Dolly muttered, remembering the strange morning when Mack found the *Iseult*, the spice that changed her life. She clucked her tongue, gently pushed the cat aside, and opened the cupboard. She'd arranged a dozen or so jars of various ingredients, most labeled, a few not, into a small spice rack. She hadn't recalled one that said *Memoria*, so she guessed it might be one of the ones with no name. "Okay, Mack, can you point it out?" Ma Tutt asked, not really expecting an answer.

Mack mewed a funny tone, trotted to the other cupboard, and pawed at that one. Dolly followed, opened it, and all three looked at the contents. Just recipe books, a few card holders, and a slew of pens and pencils. No spices.

"Your memory slipping, mister?" she chided.
*Mrrow.*

Mack jumped off the cabinet and went to the corner of the hutch next to the wall. He sniffed the

35

floor area and chirruped in anticipation a few times. Dolly got down on her hands and knees, but there was no gap large enough for a spice jar to have slipped down behind the staid piece of furniture.

"Sorry, Father. It looks like you'll have to do without. Unless you want to try out one of these unlabeled mystery spices." She got up and indicated the open cupboard door.

"With my limited baking skills, I think it best to forego any experimentation. But I trust your expert opinion. Do you think this recipe will work as is?"

"Oh, I'm quite sure it will make a scrumptious cake even without the secret spice."

"Maybe just not a *memorable* one?" The priest's eyes twinkled. Dolly laughed. Mack seemed to shake his head.

She hesitated, the card in hand. "Father, do you mind if I copy down this recipe? It looks so, um, tempting, I may want to try it out some day." A plan was forming in the back of her mind.

"By all means. I have more cards at home I can bring you, or I can simply photocopy them all and drop them by later this week."

"That would be wonderful," Dolly mumbled, already lost in the world of ingredients and ratios and serving size portions. She scribbled the instructions quickly onto another note card. After checking to make sure all the details matched, she reluctantly handed the original card back to the priest.

They walked to the front of the store. "I think

I'll go back to the parsonage and give this recipe a whirl. After my nap, that is!"

"Let me know how it goes!" Dolly said, with plans to do the same as soon as her guest was gone. Minus the nap.

"I'll be sure to bring you some tomorrow…if it turns out decent enough." Father Aguilera waved goodbye.

"I want a piece no matter what," Dolly replied as she hit the lights and locked the front door. She hurried back into the kitchen, leaving Mack with a slight case of whiplash. "Now, which one is *Memoria*?" she muttered under her breath as she stood in front of the selection of spices that Martía had evidently left behind.

Mack jumped onto the cabinet's countertop and wedged himself between Dolly and the open cupboard.

"Hey, silly. Not now, I'm working." The cat offered a throaty grumble. "I'll feed you a snack in a minute." She picked him up and set him down on the floor, though he was squirming and yowling the whole time. "What has gotten into you, mister?"

But the cat's odd behavior was quickly forgotten as she took each of the unlabeled spices and opened the jars to smell and sample.

"Hmm, this one seems right. Reminds me of mulled cider. I think it will complement the other spices nicely. If it's *Memoria*, all the better." She put it on the counter and rubbed her hands together like a mad chemist. "We'll find out soon enough, right Mack?"

The gray tabby didn't answer and Dolly was too engrossed gathering supplies to worry that he was gone. Mack was an independent soul and would come and go as he pleased, though if she called for him in the mornings he usually came trotting up in hopes of being fed. He sometimes waited for her outside by the back door, being both an indoor and outdoor cat. When she first bought the Hut, she noticed that the back entrance had a kitty door built into it. At first, she was worried about small animals being able to enter the bakery, but the door actually had a lever on it that Mack worked in order to enter and exit the building. He was one smart feline!

She put all the ingredients she needed in order to make the Memory Cake in a travel basket and headed out the back door to her car. This recipe she would attempt at home. She had a feeling something special was going to happen and she didn't want to be disturbed by some hungry customer who couldn't read a Closed sign.

Dolly was eager to get home. She lived in a small homey cabin a few miles north of Sugar Pine Station on a byway just off State Route 222. The pine trees were thick and a slender stream, no more than a crick, really, bubbled alongside the winding road to her property. The peaceful isolation invigorated her. She turned up the single lane path to her home—paved, but just barely!—and saw that she had a visitor waiting, sitting on her front stoop.

Donovan Huckly! What in the world?

She parked her car, set the parking brake, and rolled down the window. She wasn't quite ready to exit her vehicle.

He rose to greet her. "Mrs. Tutt, sorry to bother you at home. I figured since I was out hiking, it would be easier for me to meet you here than back at the Hut. I know you don't like to discuss possible city code violations when you're busy serving customers."

Dolly gritted her teeth. She didn't like discussing very much at all with Mr. City Code Enforcer. She slowly opened the car door and got out. "I'm not sure this is the best time or place to hold any kind of conversation, Mr. Huckly. I'm guessing that you, being aware of code violations and all, don't need a reminder that you're on private property."

Donovan's face grew red. "Again, I apologize, ma'am. I just thought you might want to know...."

"Know what?" Her mind raced, trying to guess what would bring this nosey inspector to her doorstep. If this was about Mack again, she'd just have to set him straight once and for all.

"Well, I'm not acting in any official capacity, mind you. I've not been appointed to the Eco-Geological Committee as of yet. But I am working on my certification for Land and Resource Management, after which I hope to persuade Mayor Tompkins that I would be perfect for..."

"Mr. Huckly! What are you getting at?"

"Oh, sorry. You see, I was exploring the mountainside behind the Hut—with your permission, mind you—when I made some interesting discoveries."

She waited and sighed. He'd tell the story his own way, but it sure was difficult to control her patience.

"Yes, yes, some very interesting discoveries. Did you know the slope behind your bakery is shifting?"

She stared at him, blank faced.

"Oh yes! Shifting. The ground is moving. The mountain's closing in. Not very fast, of course, but I'd say in the next, oh, twenty years or so, the hillside behind your bakery will start pushing in that back wall. It'll begin to crush it. Smash it. Flatten it. Eventually the whole building will succumb to the powerful gravitational forces that cause mountainsides the world over to crumble from their majestic heights to valleys below." Donovan stared off into the distance, probably awaiting some round of applause from nature itself.

Birds chirped instead.

"In the next twenty years or so?" Dolly was not impressed. "Mr. Huckly, I want to thank you for your concern, but it sounds like the danger is not imminent." She raised an eyebrow and received a reluctant shrug of agreement from her visitor. "And since, as you mentioned, this isn't an official notice from the Eco-Friendly—"

"Eco-Geological."

"—Eco-Geological Committee, I suggest you, um, mind your own business."

Donovan snapped his head back as if he'd been slapped. "Why, Mrs. Tutt. There is no need to be rude. I was simply doing you the courtesy of informing you of a very serious matter. I'm certain you are aware of the many landslides that have occurred north of us? One never knows when something like that might happen in our own back yard. So to speak."

Somehow, Dolly got the uneasy feeling that her annoying visitor had just uttered a veiled threat. She couldn't see what the point of it all was, however. She did know that she was getting tired of the rigmarole. Trying her best to suppress her irritation, she simply said, "Well, I thank you for your concern. Now if you don't mind?" She tossed her head slightly toward the driveway.

He took the hint and left. Legs weak, she leaned against the car and let out a pent up breath. Mercy! It was moments like these she wished Mack was a house cat instead of a store cat. She definitely needed a sympathetic ear every now and then. Especially when perturbed.

She thought of the elderly priest. He was certainly a good listener. But maybe he was paid to be. Dolly wasn't keen on organized religion. She'd been that route as a youngster when she, as part of a large family troupe, occupied two whole pews every time the church doors opened. Sunday school, church camp, youth choir, she'd experienced it all, and for the most part was grateful for her upbringing. It just didn't fit her anymore. Most of her siblings still attended services and her parents, now in their 90s, were active chapel-goers at their retirement village. Other than weddings and funerals, Dolly hadn't darkened the door of a sanctuary in almost twenty years.

Still a bit agitated, she entered her home, made a beeline for the kitchen and started prepping for an hour of baking. This would take her mind off the likes of Donovan Huckly. Plus, she was hoping to test a theory. These recipes were special somehow, she was sure of it. It wouldn't take long before she unlocked the secret of this one. If it proved to be successful, like those unusual doughnuts she'd made, she'd add it to her morning selection at the Hut.

In fact, as soon as she was able, she'd go through all of the recipe cards the previous owner had left behind. There were some winners in there, she was certain. Thoughts of increased business and culinary awards and maybe even a feature article about her in *Martha Stewart Living* danced like sugar plum fairies above her head.

Putting on a fresh apron, she got busy after preheating the oven. First she whisked most of the dry ingredients together and mixed the liquid elements separately. Then she beat the softened butter into the flour mix until pebble-sized clumps began to form. She added milk, stirred; added sugar, stirred some more. The mixture was smooth and waiting for the mystery spice. A quarter teaspoon was what the recipe called for, and though she wasn't certain the ingredient was *Memoria*, she knew enough to heed the directions, at least when it came particular measurements.

After pouring the batter into a greased pan, she put it in the oven and set the timer for thirty-five minutes. Suddenly exhausted, she left the kitchen and wandered to the couch in her cozy den. The windows were open, but the room was somewhat warm...the scent of fresh pine was soothing. She'd take a few moments to rest...just a ten minute nap on the sofa. She settled back...she adjusted a pillow...she was fast asleep.

The timer went off, startling her awake. The cake! She hoped it wasn't overdone. She rushed into the kitchen and found herself staring at the new industrial oven she'd had installed at the Hut. She quickly looked around. She was *at* the Hut. The lights were on, the oven was warm. She opened the oven door but there was nothing inside. Bewildered, she turned the oven off and called for Mack. No response.

A familiar clatter of fork and plate drew her to the dining room where a man sat at the counter finishing a piece of spice cake.

"Its verra good, I'll have another piece."

It was Tommy Fairbanks, one of the first customers to try her Irresistible Doughnuts, and editor of the weekly *Sugar Pine Station Bulletin*. He hadn't been back since that crazy day a number of weeks before, probably too embarrassed by his behavior to face Dolly again. But there he sat, at the counter commenting with his mouth full about the quality of her baking. At least his current review was positive; plus he'd kept the bizarre incident out of the paper.

Just then a deep rumble caused them both to look around. The room began to lurch and the kitchen door started swinging back and forth. Both coffee urns tumbled over, spilling hot dark liquid on the floor. Tommy fell from his stool and Ma grabbed the counter to keep from ending up on her keister. Tables and chairs skittered across the dining room and a loud screech echoed from the back of the bakery.

As best she could, Dolly pushed her way into the kitchen. It was like hiking uphill in an avalanche. Once past the swinging door, she screamed in alarm. The mountainside itself was pushing through the back wall. It was crushing the wooden cabinet, smashing everything it tumbled upon, flattening equipment and appliances and anything else in its path. A mountain slide was destroying the Hut. She had to escape!

Rushing to the front of the store, she saw Tommy back at the counter helping himself to another piece of spice cake.

"We have to get out of here," Ma yelled. "This is no time to stop and eat!"

"It's—"

"Yes, I know, it's very good! But we have to go!" She pulled at Tommy's arm.

The phone rang. Dolly ignored it. She pulled at Tommy again, glancing in panic through the service window at the advancing face of rock. The mountain was ready to break through into the dining area. The mounted telephone rang again and with the next rumble of moving earth, the receiver jumped out of its cradle.

Tommy picked it up and said, "Hello?" He listened for a moment. "It's for you."

Dolly stared at him, wide-eyed, hysterical. He handed her the phone. As if in a trance, she took it. The mountain rumbled. The ground shook. Tommy picked up his plate and took another bite of cake. She straightened her apron and squeaked out something even she couldn't understand.

Then more firmly, "Hello, Ma Tutt's Donu...I mean...."

Ma whirled around. Tommy Fairbanks was gone. The mountain was gone. In the blink of an eye, the Hut was gone. She was standing in the doorway between her den and kitchen, back at home. Safe. Sound. The floor beneath her feet was solid. Grabbing a nearby chair, she collapsed into it and found she was holding the phone.

She raised it to her lips. "Hello? Um, Ma Tutt speaking." She barely had breath to huff a strand of gray hair out of her face. The dream, the hallucination, whatever it was, was over.

"Oh, Mrs. Tutt, Father Aguilera here. I thought I had the answering machine, but I'm glad to speak with you directly."

"Yes, Father, I just, er, woke up from a nap...I think. Is anything wrong?" Her knuckles were white from gripping the receiver. Like at the Hut, she had a landline at home as her cell phone didn't get that great a reception this far from civilization. But she seldom got calls at her residence, other than from her family in the valley. This was the first time the priest had telephoned.

"Oh, sorry to wake you. But no, nothing's wrong. I just thought you'd be interested to know I found it."

Dolly couldn't think. "Found what?"

"The spice. To make the Memory Cake."

"*Memoria*?"

"Yes! When I went into my office I opened the file drawer where I keep the recipes Martía Cooper gave me. You'd never guess. A small jar seemed to be just waiting for me there in one of my hanging files. The label tells me it's the very ingredient we need. Very strange."

*Strange. You want to talk about strange!* The priest had no idea. He'd probably misplaced the spice, anyway. The man was in his late seventies, at least. Maybe his memory was going. She stopped a rising hysteria and giggled. The cake might do him good.

Gaining a bit of composure, she said, "Wonderful. I do hope your kitchen experiment will be a success." She cringed at her word choice. She made a mental note not to experiment with unlabeled ingredients ever again.

There was a pause on the other end of the line. It sounded as if the priest muffled the phone. Dolly heard a bit of a one-way conversation and then Father Aguilera came through again loud and clear. "I hope you don't think I'm being a bother, but I was wondering if you'd consider coming over and helping me bake a cake." Another pause. "I wouldn't normally suggest it, except that…well, Mack is here and somewhat insists I extend the invitation. He's been wanting me to call you all afternoon."

Dolly pulled the receiver away from her ear and stared at it. She blinked and shook her head. She replaced it, crooking it between her head and shoulder, then wiped her hands nervously on the fabric of her apron. "I'm sorry?"

"Mack dropped by the parsonage and woke me up from my nap. He led me to my office where I found the spice. And now he wants us to make the Memory Cake."

"He told you all this." Her feline friend certainly could carry on a conversation of meows and yowls, and Dolly often imagined she understood what he was saying, but this was a bit rich even for her. "Well, I…oh, why not? Let me freshen up, put on a new apron, and I'll be right over."

Despite what had just happened to her—and her

reservations about the priest's state of mind—Dolly was determined to press on. She was certain now this cake just had to be made. If Mrs. Cooper's recipes turned out the way they were intended, then surely it would be for everyone's benefit, right? The Hut would stay busy, obviously, but really it was all about the customers! Serve the people!

She almost convinced herself that that was the reason she was heading over to help the priest. But in the back of her mind, she wondered if she was tempting fate. With a shrug, she decided to carry on. What did she have to lose by trying the recipe again? It certainly couldn't come out any worse than her first attempt. Could it?

Finally back in her kitchen, Dolly took the cake out of the oven and tossed it in the trash without a second thought. If she'd had hallucinations from the aroma alone, Lord knows what would happen if she tasted it. She took a marker and immediately labeled that mystery spice *Nightmare*!

Within twenty minutes she was pulling into a parking space in front of the church's rectory. St. Anne's was one of only three churches in the small community of Sugar Pine Station. There was a Baptist congregation up the mountain a ways and a Federated Church in the middle of what could be considered downtown. A block away and on the other side of the street was the Catholic Church. Definitely within walking distance of the Hut, especially for a cat who liked to roam.

Mack greeted her, along with Father Aguilera, at the open door to his humble home. The parsonage was connected to the main building via the parish office where the solitary priest devoted himself to his studies and to prayer. He was the sexton, secretary, and celebrant all wrapped into one. It was a small parish.

"Thank you for coming," he said, leading the way inside. It was a partly sunny late afternoon and a slight breeze made its way through the small business district, bringing with it the scent of pine and possible evening rain. So refreshing! The priest left the door open to allow the soothing mountain air do its divinely guided duty.

Dolly looked over the small kitchen and returned a smile when the priest showed her all that he'd done in preparation for her visit. Mixing bowls, measuring cups, and the many ingredients were standing at the ready. A quaint, purple jar punctuated the procession. She made sure the label read *Memoria*. It did. *Whew!*

"I have to admit, I'm curious. And a bit surprised. Mack seems to have taken quite a liking to you. Now don't get me wrong. I'm not jealous; cats own humans, of course, and not the other way around. But it just never occurred to me that he ever left the area around the Hut, though of course it's normal for cats to wander their territory, I suppose."

Father Aguilera coughed and looked a bit embarrassed. "I hope you'll forgive me, but I'm afraid I'm guilty of the sin of omission when it comes to my relationship with Mack." Dolly looked at him in confusion. "You see, I've neglected to tell you that we go back quite a few years." He took on a wistful look. "Quite a few years, indeed," he added, somewhat to himself.

"Mack belongs to you?" Dolly asked, a bit of disappointment edging her voice.

"Cat's don't belong to anyone. Didn't you just say that?" The priest chuckled. "No, he's just a good friend. Before you bought the Hut, he'd drop by the parish every few days and check in on me. Though I suspect he was just as happy to see a bowl of food as he was me, isn't that right, Mister Gato?"

Mack *mrreowed* as if the ponderings of human beings were simply too banal to contemplate.

Dolly's mood brightened. "That makes sense. Mack seems much too independent for anyone to consider him anything less than a 'cat about town.'"

To this Mack agreed with a throaty yowl. He then nudged the legs of both his humans as if to get them moving. They shook their heads and smiled. Time to start baking.

After they rehearsed the recipe and dove into more of the prep work, the priest asked, "So what brings you to Sugar Pine Station. I understand you're semi-retired, but a bakery is quite an undertaking at any age, if you'll pardon the unintended implication. Surely there's a story behind your move to the mountains."

"It is definitely an undertaking, and yes,

especially at my age," Ma replied, washing her hands and toweling off the excess water. "But no offense taken. I'm almost sixty and decided that before I got too old I'd fulfill a dream of owning my own business. A corporate time clock owned me for more than thirty years, and though I did well financially, I'd finally had enough. Since I've basically baked my way through life during my spare time—contributing quite extensively to the waistlines of my family and friends, let me tell you—it seemed natural for me to open a pastry shop."

"So you can contribute now to all of our waistlines?" the priest mockingly accused. "I see how you are." He shook his finger at her in exaggerated reprimand.

"No one's forcing that bear claw on you, Father," Dolly said, laughing. "I remember early on, my young nieces and nephews begged me to make cakes in the shape of Mickey Mouse or Daisy Duck. Then it was Strawberry Shortcake and the Teenage Mutant Ninja Turtles. I did a Bart Simpson cake one time but drew the line at Beavis and Butt-head." Dolly tapped a spatula on the rim of a bowl to emphasize her point. "Now that most of my brothers' and sisters' children are in college, I've switched from cakes to postal service friendly goods. In fact, I just sent my niece Amy some fancy cookies and chocolate covered truffles. It's been so much fun, especially when they Skype me so I can see them open their goodie boxes."

Her grin was wide and her eyes were laughing. Father Aguilera remarked, "You've been truly blessed."

She thought about the easy and sincere comment. Blessed. In the past it was only so much spiritual jargon. But on the lips of this kind and self-effacing minister, it seemed appropriate. True, even. The grin remained. Yes, she supposed she had been blessed.

"Tell me about yourself, Father. What brought you to this community?" She'd heard the local gossip, but to finally hear it from the man himself definitely piqued her interest.

"Not a very long story. I arrived the summer of 1959, and yes I know, that makes me very old." He chuckled as he started mixing the dry ingredients into a large bowl. "It was a sweltering week; we were in the middle of a heat wave. I hated the mountains for that reason. The weather is hot and dry one day and wet and rainy the next. I preferred my coastal home in northern California. Always temperate. Plus the winding roads! I get carsick fairly easily and I remember having panic attacks once I learned I'd been appointed to serve the parish of St. Anne. My hope and prayer was to return to Eureka within a few years."

"But you never did." This was the unusual part, for even she knew most priests didn't stay very long in one church.

"That's right. St. Anne's is my first and only

ministerial assignment. Fifty-five years ago next month. I've enjoyed almost every minute."

Dolly did the math. Assuming he was in his early twenties when he began serving, Father Emilio Aguilera would now be in his late seventies. Not too old, really. The longer one lives, the more one realizes age is mostly a state of mind. Didn't her sister tell her that sixty was the new fifty? She rubbed her back and flexed her arthritic fingers. *Hmm. That one's a bit hard to swallow.* She looked at their progress. The batter was almost ready. The oven was pre-heating. Mack was supervising.

"One more spice to go," the determined priest declared.

"Only a quarter teaspoon," the experienced baker reminded. "Trust me, you want to follow Martía's directions to the letter."

"Sounds like another story in there somewhere."

"Oh, one or two, most definitely. Remind me to tell them to you some day. Their memory is a bit too fresh!"

Father Aguilera chuckled and mixed in the final ingredient. He then poured the batter into the nine by thirteen cake pan that Dolly had already greased. They both admired their experiment a moment longer before ushering it into the welcoming oven.

"I'll set the timer," Ma said.

"I'll make us some coffee," the Father replied.

And while they waited, more stories of their past surfaced and found their way to eager and appreciative ears. Even Mack seemed to pay attention to the unfolding history of his two good friends. They reminisced about their high school years—both of their Senior Trips were to San Francisco—and college and young adult experiences. Emilio Aguilera was a sly and witty story teller and Dolly laughed after every punch line. For her part, the wonderful memories she shared were detailed and charming and the priest responded with encouraging nods and smiles.

So deep in conversation were they that when the timer went off they both jumped in surprise. The kitchen fragrances had relaxed them to a point they'd forgotten why they were there. Nutmeg and ginger, cinnamon and allspice, cloves and some other tangy mouthwatering aroma, along with coffee and sunshine, mountain air and friendship filled the parsonage and spilled out into the surrounding downtown.

Ma sprang up and checked the cake in the oven. It was perfect! She removed the cake pan to let it cool, poured both of them a cup of coffee, and returned to the kitchen table for another round of stories.

A knock at the door and calls of hello from a couple of friendly voices announced the arrival of Jo and Kelli, best friends and workout partners. Most days the two women could be seen running in and around Sugar Pine Station; and they almost always wore their exercise outfits whether they were running or not.

"I hope we aren't intruding," said Jo. "The door was wide open."

"And I hope we aren't dressed too informally," added Kelli. "This being a church and all."

"But the smells!" they both said together. "What are you baking?"

Father Aguilera stood to greet them and offered them both chairs. "We were just about to have a piece of spice cake. Would you care to join us?"

"Do runners run?" said Jo.

"Do cake lovers eat cake?" added Kelli.

The four of them laughed and Ma Tutt got up to serve them all a piece of the special dessert. Ma knew the ladies from the doughnut shop and the priest knew just about everyone, it seemed. They settled themselves around the table.

"Hey in there! Father, are you home?" boomed another voice from just outside the parsonage.

"Better cut another slice," the priest said to Dolly as Big Benjamin Reed pressed his way into the kitchen with an infectious grin on his face. He removed his cap and let the tangled mess of unruly hair flow naturally about his face, which sported a beard worthy of a song. Big Ben was a mountain of a man and looked the part. If another casting call for *Grizzly Adams* went out, he'd surely be in the running.

Though Ma had heard about Ben Reed, she'd never met him, as he rarely made trips to town, preferring the peace and quiet of his mountain hideaway accessible only by foot and that after a two hour trek. Father Aguilera made introductions. "In town for your annual grocery shopping?" he teased.

"I venture in about twice a month, thank you— whether I need to or not. I'm not quite that uncivilized." He winked at Jo and Kelli, who both blushed.

The five of them squeezed around the table and coffee was poured. A fresh pot was set to brewing and cake was served. Everyone had their fork at the ready.

"What are we eating?" Big Ben asked.

"A new recipe called Memory Cake," replied the priest. "A spice cake that I couldn't have made without Ma's help." From the other room a cat meowed. "Nor Mack's," he added, apologetically. "Our kitty helper is a bit shy when it comes to people, but evidently not when it comes to recognition." Another meow, possibly a reprimand.

"Smells delicious," said Jo. They all dug in. "Tastes delicious," added Kelli. "Still warm, just the way I like it." "So moist, it melts in your mouth." "Burst of flavors." "Wonderful." The two went on like this for a few moments until Kelli put down her fork with an *Mm Mm Mmm*.

"You call this Memory Cake?" she asked. "It definitely brings back memories of helping my mother bake things when I was a child." Jo nodded in agreement.

Big Ben said, "It may surprise you, but I remember helping my ma when I was little too. Except we had an outdoor kitchen, a brick oven, and a wood pit for grilling."

"Sounds rustic," Dolly said, "but charming."

"Oh, it was perfect," Ben replied. He launched into a rambling, culinary tale of mountain cooking, backwoods adventures, and family recipes—both the favorites and the failures. Everyone groaned at the mention of Skunk Stew and Squirrel Kabobs. And they were shocked to hear of Ben's first encounter with Elderberry Wine. He'd quaffed five cups before his ma knew what was happening. He was five at the time, "And a drunk child telling stories around the campfire is evidently a hoot. My Pa was laughing so hard he didn't have the heart to tan my hide. Ma never saw the humor in it, however, so had no inhibitions about setting me straight with a willow switch."

Another round of cake and coffee brought more stories from Kelli, Jo, Ma, and Father Aguilera. The five chatted and chortled and cheered each other on until the cake and coffee had disappeared. After about an hour, they all sat back with contented sighs.

"What a lovely way to spend the afternoon," Ma Tutt declared. "Thank you, Father, for inviting me over."

"And for allowing us to drop in unannounced," Jo said on behalf of the other two. They all got up and helped straighten as best they could, though the space was a bit cramped with Big Ben in the mix.

Soon the three serendipitous guests made their way out the door with a series of sincere *Thank yous*, *Good to see yous*, and *See you laters*.

When they were alone, and after Mack returned from the other room, Dolly helped her host finish cleaning up. "That really was a wonderful trip down memory lane," she said. "I wonder if our secret ingredient had anything to do with it, or if we'd have shared the same stories regardless."

"Does it matter?" asked the priest.

Dolly thought about it. She considered her half-baked plans to increase her business with those mysterious recipes and decided she didn't really need a magical cake to help her become more successful after all. In fact, she was fortunate to be doing so well already. Blessed, even.

*Memoria.* She thought about her wonderful childhood years in the church. She reflected on her decades in corporate America. She considered her wonderful extended family and all the treats she'd made for them. And she smiled.

"No, I suppose the particular spice really doesn't matter. There's a certain magic that occurs anytime friends share a meal and a memory, don't you think?"

Father Aguilera nodded, another twinkle in his eye. "I know just what you mean."

Mack *mrrowed* his agreement as well.

## 'Tail' Number Three
### Birthday Surprise

Ma Tutt unlocked the doughnut shop and called out, "Morning, Mack."

No response.

Of course, Mac wouldn't call out, being a cat and all, but even so Dolly expected a welcoming mew or two. It was breakfast time, after all.

"Mack," she called again after straightening up out front. She entered the kitchen, flipped on the lights, found her apron and was just about to put it on when she spied a gray fluff curled up in the corner, practically hidden behind the huge, ugly hutch that served as a storage cabinet. A full bowl of food, untouched from the night before, waited nearby.

"Oh my!" Dolly tossed her apron on the counter and quickly knelt down beside the tabby. Hesitating but for a moment, she gently petted Mack's side. His fur was dull and without the velvety touch she'd

59

become so familiar with. Upon her gentle stroking, the gray mackerel raised his head slightly and let out a pathetic mew.

"What's wrong, Mack? Sick to the stomach? Eat too many day olds?" Her poor attempt at humor was met with a dismissive feline sigh and Mack laid his head back down. His breathing seemed labored and Dolly felt his heart racing as she picked him up and held him close.

"I'm taking you to Doc Moore's right away," she mumbled, then realized it was a little after four in the morning, her usual time to arrive and prepare the day's offerings. She glanced at the kitchen clock. "Oh dear. Well, I hope he doesn't mind a wake-up call!"

With that, she grabbed her apron, gently wrapped Mack into a makeshift sling, and with him bundled like a baby, Dolly turned out the lights and made for the front door. Making sure the sign said Closed, she locked the Hut and headed two blocks down Main Street to Dr. Gerald Moore's Veterinary Clinic.

Gerry Moore was also a semi-retired transplant from the San Joaquin Valley. He'd had a thriving practice in Fresno but high blood pressure and a nagging cough known as Valley Fever convinced him he needed a change of pace and climate. Plus, the five years of loneliness following the death of his wife of twenty-four wonderful years had finally gotten to him. He moved to Sugar Pine Station, an old logger's camp that had its heyday during the late 1800s when narrow gauge railways were the only means in and out of the surrounding mountains. Back then, the pristine forest was thick with timber for a rapidly expanding nation and fed an aggressive building boom around the San Francisco bay about 150 miles due west. The forest was once again pristine, but now held a fascinating history that occupied Doc Moore on his days off.

He was accustomed to getting up early, the animals kenneled in his clinic demanded it, but 4:15 antemeridian was a tad early even for him. So when the banging started in soon after the doorbell ringing ceased, Gerry, foggy-eyed, made his way downstairs. He lived above his office in an apartment, a typical two-story building that could be found on any number of Main Streets across America.

"Just a gall-durned minute," he called as he switched on the lights of the small reception area. Through the glass door he could see a woman holding a bundle as if it were a baby at the breast. He could feel his blood pressure on the rise. Emergencies. Another reason he'd left Fresno for higher elevations. But what did he expect? Pets rarely waited for office hours to get sick.

Unlocking the door, he barely had a chance to step out of the way before Dolores Tutt—he recognized her now—rushed in, puffing stray strands of graying hair out of her eyes. She wasn't unpleasant to look at, he thought, a bit thick around the middle, but aging well. He chastised himself for even going there. They were both around sixty, after all. And both taking the natural route to old age, avoiding hair dye and, in Dolly's case, make up. Still, she possessed a kind of long-term beauty that only enhanced with time....

He shook his head to clear his thoughts. She mistook the gesture and began to plead, "Please, you just have to see Mack. He's dying, I just know it!"

"Now, now, I'll see him. Let's not jump to conclusions."

He took the bundle, unwrapped the gray tabby and trundled off down the hall as he began a running dialog with Mack and Dolly, though he wasn't necessarily looking for a response. *Let's check you over, little buddy.* Dolly followed him into an exam room. *You're a handsome one, aren't ya?* Mack mewed in response. He was soon weighed—*thirteen pounds, a bit overweight for his size*—and then gently poked and prodded. He checked the cat's teeth. *Hmm. You need a good cleaning.* Another mew. A few more minutes of *hmms* and *ohs* and an *ah yes*, Dr. Moore sighed and announced his verdict.

"Kidneys are struggling, I'm guessing."

Dolly looked at him, eyes wide. "Is that serious?"

"Yes, but I think you brought him here in time. He's dehydrated, so I'll run an IV, of course. Put him on some meds and in a couple of days, if all goes well, he should be close to normal."

"What if all does not go well?"

Gerry lowered his voice and turned away from Mack as if he didn't want the cat to overhear. "Well, kidney failure leads to other organs shutting down and we'll have a decision to make."

Dolly gasped. Though she'd only known Mack less than six months, she'd come to love him as if he'd always been in her life. He was a generic tom with a mackerel pattern, which gave rise to his name as he had no identifying collar when she first purchased the Hut. And he had just the right blend of affection and independence for Dolly's personality. She enjoyed his company even though she cursed with affection when he sometimes got under foot.

"No! We can't…"

"Now, now. Let's just wait and see, shall we? Cross that bridge when we come to it." Gerry patted her shoulder gently, a shoulder tight with tension as well as muscle toned from years of kitchen work.

She looked at him with grateful eyes. "Of course."

"I'll keep him here in the meantime. Nothing for you to do but drop in for a visit later this afternoon or tomorrow. Why don't you go back to the Hut and open up. I'm sure you have customers wondering why they can't get their morning fix of sugar and grease." He indicated the clock with a nod.

Dolly turned and stared at the time. It was just after five o'clock. "Oh my! They'll be lined up down the block." She went to Mack, lying feebly on the exam table. "I'll be back this afternoon, okay dear kitty?" He blinked without lifting his head. She patted it before she left the room.

As Gerry and Dolly made their way to the front door, the vet tried to assure her but was cautious with his words. "He should respond to the antibiotics, but I have to tell you, it'll be tough for him...he's in his golden years."

"How can you tell his age?"

"Condition of his teeth, mostly. I'd say he's a ways past fifteen, maybe close to twenty years old. A normal age span for a cat like him. His time may be at hand. I just wanted to prepare you for the possibility."

Dolly deflated. A heavy sigh escaped her lips, but she shook the doctor's hand and said, "Thank you. I'll be back this afternoon. Do everything you can for Mack, he's...he's a friend."

"I understand. And I certainly will do everything I can to help the little critter get back on his feet."

Gerry closed the door behind her, locked up, and turned out the lights for a few more hours. The clinic was open 10 to 3. He was semi-retired after all, though he was always willing to help out in emergencies. Plus, he had a soft spot in his heart for cats. He returned Dolly's wave as she headed up the street.

The line was indeed half-way down the block when Ma Tutt returned to the Hut and opened the door for business. There were gentle teasings as she made her way through her crowd of regulars. "Thought you'd left us, Ma!" "Where were you, at the Creamy Pie eating breakfast?" This brought a few chuckles. Everyone knew she hated the franchise across the street with a passion.

"Sorry, folks," she said as she entered first. "Domestic emergency." The bells jingled and her many customers followed her into the cozy coffee shop.

She hit the lights and hurried behind the counter to arrange yesterday's few remaining pastries and set out four trays of doughnuts she'd prepared the night before. Almost fresh at the Hut was always fresher than across the street. Fortunately, she'd started the coffee first thing that morning, so the aroma, which mingled with mountain pine and fresh air, relaxed the anxious crowd.

To her regulars she said, "I'll have a greater selection later this morning, but for now," she turned her attention to the first person in line, "what can I get you?" It was then she noticed who was standing before her. "Oh, it's you." She was tempted to say, "Next."

At the counter, with his ever-present clipboard at the ready, was Donovan Huckly, the thirty-something Inspector General for the village of Sugar Pine Station. Depending on the color of his work shirt, he was at different times the Animal Control Officer, Utility Compliance, and General Pain-in-the-Butt. He'd been appointed by the mayor himself, he often reminded anyone who cared to listen.

Dolly disliked him and for good reason. He'd tried to shut her down by turning off her electricity and then the next day wanted to remove Mack from the premises. Fortunately, those issues had been resolved. He'd then tried to frighten her by insinuating the mountainside behind her business was shifting and would eventually crush the Hut! What could it be now?

"Hello, Mrs. Tutt," Donovan said amiably enough. He was wearing a steel gray work shirt, a color she didn't readily associate with one of his many governmental roles. As usual, his name was emblazoned above the pocket. Underneath, however, was a new tag line, at least to her: *Building Inspector.*

"Mr. Huckly." She gave him an icy stare. "One doughnut or two this morning." She knew he wasn't there for breakfast, but she'd never again give him the satisfaction of being intimidated by his 'professional capacity.'

"Oh, I'm here in my professional capacity this morning. So no doughnuts today. I will, however, have a cup of your fine, delicious coffee. It's still pay what you wish, I assume?"

"No, sir. You can still help yourself, but put a dollar in the jar; fifty cents for a refill." She nodded at the coffee station. Being a one woman shop, she decided to train her customers to do for themselves in the caffeine department. Most of her regulars even cleaned their tables when they were done and straightened the newspapers they were leaving behind.

"Oh, well, that works too. But I also need to speak with you. It's a matter of extreme importance."

Father Emilio Aguilera, a fan of Ma Tutt's pastries and one of her most faithful customers, shuffled close and whispered a word to Donovan. Despite his advanced age and diminutive stature, the priest could muster quite a presence when needed. This was evidently such a time and Mr. Huckly nervously looked around and then announced, "I see that you're quite busy, so I'll just drink my coffee and wait for a break in the action."

Wonderful.

"Oh, and I think I'll have one of those old fashioned doughnuts right there." He pointed at a specific pastry in the second tray behind the glass. "No, that one." Dolly took a piece of waxed paper and removed the chosen one, evidently predestined to be eaten by Donovan Huckly before the foundation of the world, and handed it to him. She took his money and with a relieved smile, greeted the priest.

"The usual, Father?"

With a wink and a nod, the elder minister accepted a bear claw on a plate along with two pats of butter. As he turned to go, he paused and said, "Mack will be back in no time, no need to worry about his illness."

Startled, Dolly paused, an offered fork in mid-air. "How did you know Mack was sick? I just took him to Dr. Moore's this morning."

"Oh yes, I know. I saw you rushing out of his office just now." He winked again and took the utensil she was holding. "There are, however, some other secrets that both cats and the Church share, you know," he said cryptically before shuffling off to get his coffee and a cushy seat by the window.

Dolly blinked in confusion. The demands of the next customer in line, however, snapped her out of what little reflection she could devote to Mack, and she got busy serving the rest of the early morning rush. During quick breaks she prepared the rest of the day's baked goods and finally, by mid-morning was able to come from behind the counter and check on the tables and chairs. Most were clean and orderly, as usual, and she sat down for a moment to rest her weary feet. The priest had already left, but Donovan was still there nursing a coffee.

"What do you want?" she asked without pre-amble.

"I need to inspect your basement," he responded with equal terseness.

"I don't have a basement. I'm not even sure if I have an attic. What you see is what you get." She indicated the sitting area, prep area, kitchen, and back storage room with a sweep of an arm.

"I have examined the original architectural blueprint of this building and know for a fact that it has a basement. I've come to inspect the foundation. Make sure it isn't deteriorating, in which case I'd have to issue an order to vacate the facility until the structure can be secured."

So there it was. Another attempt at closing her business. At least he was transparent about his purposes. But why? What did she ever do to get on his bad side?

"You don't happen to work for Creamy Pie across the street, do you?"

"Mrs. Tutt, you know good and well that I've been duly appointed by the good mayor of Sugar Pine Station to handle many of the routine jobs that keep our quaint mountain community, well, quaint. This building has had its problems since it was built in 1938. I've done my research. We want to make sure it's safe for occupation and business."

Ah yes, the royal we. Dolly pursed her lips. Donovan was right about the building having some issues. It was a log cabin-like structure that had a mountain slope for a backyard and sat at the north end of town on State Route 222. The narrow two-lane route was a backwoods pass to Yosemite National Park and the Hut was a familiar sight to summer travelers on their way to some crystal clear lakes and sparkling rivers rushing with snowmelt waters. Unfortunately, it had stood empty off and on for a number of years allowing wild varmints and weather to take their toll.

But for some unknown reason, Donovan Huckly was trying to evict her from the premises. Maybe he wanted the building for himself. Well, two could play at this game.

"Some say the place is haunted," she offered.

"Or cursed," he replied.

"I've not had bad luck with it."

Donovan raised his eyebrows.

"Well, other than the incident which led to the remodel. But surely that proves the place is safe. Insurance wouldn't have paid had it not passed building code."

"They didn't know about the basement."

"Well, let's just go try and find this mysterious cellar of yours," she said as she got up and led the way through the swinging door and into the kitchen. "Look around. There is nothing here but a storage room off to the left and a back door to the right which leads to the dumpster and my parking spot on the side of the Hut. The mountain, of course, is directly behind the building." She pointed to the wall where the monster cabinet sat.

The old hutch, weathered with age and use, was probably left behind by the previous owners, a mysterious Gypsy couple by the name of Cooper. It was so huge and heavy, she doubted it had been moved since originally placed where it was. It housed old cookbooks and stacks of papers, a spice rack, some pens and pencils, and most importantly, a slew of index cards scrawled with barely legible recipes. These she was going through slowly and typing them into her new computer that she bought herself as a reward for quitting her job in the valley and moving to the mountains.

Donovan entered the storage room, a fairly good sized walk-in, to have a look around. Dolly was about to follow when she noticed the cabinet was off. It was out from the corner, eight to ten inches or so away from the wall. That was where she'd found Mack earlier this morning. She'd been too distraught over the cat's ailing health that she'd completely failed to notice that the hutch was not in its normal spot. *But it couldn't have moved!*

She stared at the small space between the storage room wall and the wooden cabinet. She moved closer. She stared some more. There, just visible as it half-peeped out from under the big piece of furniture was a latch in the wooden floorboards. There was no linoleum here as whoever did the flooring—the Coopers?—simply placed the material around the cabinet. But with it away from the wall, a bit of a mystery was revealed. Barely visible in the wooden slats were lines indicating there might be a door in the floor.

Donovan emerged from the storage closet and Dolly quickly turned her back to the cabinet, hiding the gap between it and the wall.

"Well, no entrance to any basement in there. I even moved some shelves around, hope you don't mind, but you might need to rearrange your supplies once I'm gone." Huckly gave an apologetic shrug. Before Dolly could reply, his cell phone rang. He punched a button and answered, "Donovan here. Uh huh. Uh huh. Okay, will be right on it."

Dolly questioned him with a raised eyebrow.

"Black bear and her cubs wandering around the rest area south of town. Gotta put on my forest green shirt." And without further explanation turned to leave. "I'll be back though, next week. I'm busy handing out overdue utility bills and shut off notices the next few days."

That would be his dark blue shirt, Dolly thought automatically. She knew his quirky ways by now. "Take your time," Dolly mumbled, already considering who she was going to call to help push the cabinet the rest of the way off the trap door. It took only a moment's reflection. Benjamin Reed, that's who. Or Big Ben to his friends. He'd be able to move it without breaking a sweat.

The prospect of a hidden cellar excited her. Maybe they'd find something interesting. Gold maybe. Or secret documents. Surely something more intriguing than deteriorating basement walls. Well, if Mack—sick or not—had anything to do with this, then she was sure it contained its share of mysteries.

Dolly ran out of doughnuts by noon, which was typical now that she had a steady flow of business. It had taken her a few months to get to where she wasn't worried about whether she could pay her bills or not. She'd worked hard. And she'd been lucky...those 'irresistible doughnuts' had helped jumpstart her success. She thought of her attempt at baking a 'memory cake' as well—and the near disaster connected with that experience. Never again would she tamper with Martía's recipes! One shouldn't mess with magic!

She chided herself. Of course, it wasn't magic. It must have been a full moon or some weird confluence of events that caused all that craziness awhile back. But a magical cat? Surely not. A doughnut love potion spice? Nightmare in a bottle? Too ridiculous to contemplate.

So she'd pushed the matter to the back of her mind. Until now. She locked the door, turned the sign to Closed, wiped down the tables, and headed back to the kitchen to stare at the unmovable cabinet that had evidently been moved…by Mack! Dear kitty! Dolly took off her apron and hit the lights. She was at Dr. Moore's clinic within no time.

"How's my friend?" she asked as Gerry met her at the door. He led her to the kennel cages where Mack was resting. The gray tabby's front legs were shaved, giving him a funny, poodle-like appearance, and an IV was still dripping. He didn't move.

"As you can see, he's still quite sick," Dr. Moore said.

"When will he bounce back?"

The vet gently led her out of the room and they entered his office where they both took a seat. His manner was somber. She feared the worse.

"Dolly, you have to prepare yourself that Mack might not get better."

She heard the words but didn't accept their meaning. She shook her head but remained silent.

"In fact—and I hate to mention this now, but I think you should know—Father Aguilera visited

Mack earlier today."

Confusion had her wrinkling her forehead. "Oh, really? I mean, I guess that's okay. They are on pretty good terms with each other."

She thought about the aging priest and his interactions with the gray mackerel. Yes, he'd always greeted Mack every morning. Sometimes the tabby would sit on the Father's lap as he ate his bear claw, something Mack never did with any of the other customers. And, of course, she'd recently learned that the two had known each other before she'd came to town. Mack had evidently visited the priest at the parsonage on numerous occasions.

Gerry squirmed a bit in his seat. "I think I should also mention to you that I overheard the Father, er, pray over Mack."

"Well, that's not too unusual, is it? I mean, he's a priest after all. Praying is what he does for a living."

"True. But I think...although I'm not one hundred percent certain since I only caught part of the prayer—so don't quote me—but I think he was giving Mack..."

"...Giving Mack?" she prompted.

"Giving Mack his last rites."

"What?"

"Well, technically it's called a prayer of extreme unction, but I'm not an expert in Catholic doctrine, so don't quote..."

"Yes, got it, don't quote you." Dolly filed that one away for when the inevitable bill came.

*Three hundred dollars? But Dr. Moore, I won't quote you, so how about two-fifty?*

Her attempt at grim humor didn't please her any more than the unexpected news about Father Aguilera's prayer for Mack. Extreme unction, last rites, what did it matter? It could only mean one thing—Mack wasn't going to make it! Doc Moore had his doubts, now the priest!

As her confusion turned to fear, she said, "I think I need to pay the Father a visit." After another peek at Mack and a whispered *So long*, Dolly marched out of the doctor's office and stomped her way to St. Anne's Catholic Church. She was upset and she didn't know why.

Ten minutes later she was sitting in the parish office. The priest greeted her warmly, despite her cool demeanor.

"How can I help you today?" he started, a comforting smile accompanying that ever present twinkle in his eye. The office was pleasant, decorated here and there with tasteful items that didn't distract one from the gentle spirituality of the surroundings.

"I heard you went to see Mack," she said, getting right to the point, though she couldn't quite muster the anger she was holding in reserve. "I have to say, I'm not too happy about that. I heard you…" She remembered not to quote the doctor. "I mean, what were you doing there?"

Instead of answering her question, the priest templed his fingers in front of him. "How long have you known Mack?"

It wasn't an accusatory question, just a sincere inquiry. Immediately, her somewhat frosty attitude melted. She'd known Mack for only a few months but realized she'd grown to love the finicky and sometimes confounding ol' sour puss. Like anyone in her place, she didn't want to lose him.

"About six months. I first met him when the realtor showed me the Hut. He was hanging out back and I thought he was a stray. He was friendly enough, but demanding. The moment I moved in, he did as well and insisted on staying at the shop at night instead of coming home with me. There's a kitty door in the back so he comes and goes as he pleases. He's been a fixture there ever since. But then, you already knew that. The last time we visited, you mentioned you've been friends with him for a few years, is that right?"

"Indeed it is. In fact, I've known Mack for quite a few years now. He's been a fixture in this community for some time." The priest's eyes took on a faraway gaze and his tone became wistful. "His name hasn't always been Mack, of course. But he's flexible and doesn't mind that we call him that now."

Dolly chuckled. "Well, that's a relief. And just how do you know this about our beloved feline?"

"Oh, he told me the first week the Hut opened when I called him Tozier out of habit. He said you named him Mack. He likes it, so that's what I call him too."

Okay. "Um." She had no other response and reminded herself the man was pushing eighty.

"You don't believe me."

"No, no. I see you with Mack every morning, by the window in your usual spot. You're the only lap he'll jump into. Other than mine. He's a bit standoffish to the other customers, I have to admit."

"That's because we've known each other for almost fifty years."

Silence.

"Say that again?"

"Mack and I go back to the summer of 1965. I remember it well because our little Main Street officially became part of State Route 222 when they finally completed Sugar Pine Pass and connected our mountain road to the national park. We became an alternate scenic route to Yosemite. Traffic that year was horrendous and our little community grew from three hundred residents to just over a thousand in a few short years. We haven't grown much since then and the traffic has flattened out, but 1965 was a very important year for our town, yes indeed."

Dolly got the impression that, for the priest, the significance of the year was as much related to Mack's arrival as the highway's. Wait. What was she thinking? Mack couldn't have arrived fifty years ago. Cats don't live that long.

As if reading her mind, Father Aguilera said, "Cats, of course, don't live for fifty years. But Mack's an exception. He came with a bit of a mystery."

"What do you mean?" She wasn't ready to buy any of this yet, but she had learned that the priest was a pretty good story teller. So she settled in to hear what he had to say. She'd reserve judgment for later.

"Well, I told you about Rohan and Martía Cooper, right? The Gypsy couple. You may have heard a few things about Gypsies…small traveling clans that live off the land and make do by trading, selling, fixing, sometimes stealing what they can, though they aren't a bad lot. I think they prefer to be called Romany, and appear to be an ethnicity all their own. They never stay long in one place, that's the truth."

Dolly nodded. She'd actually had experience with a band of Gypsies who'd wandered their way through the Central Valley when she was a child. Her parents, farmers just scraping by themselves, had let them camp in their vineyards. They'd been friendly enough, helping with the raisin harvest at the tail end of summer. They were pretty good cooks, she recalled.

"At any rate, a few months after Route 222 officially opened in '65, this one Gypsy band arrived in Sugar Pine Station and camped south of town for a few weeks. This was an oddity for our small community and most everyone made their way to their temporary settlement to at least gawk at our unusual visitors. We found them to be cordial, if not exactly friendly, and a number of people did business with them. I even had one young family show up for mass one Sunday morning."

"Are they particularly religious?" Dolly asked. "I'd heard they were, well, heathen, if you know what I mean."

"I guess it depends on the individual," the priest replied. "If I'm not mistaken, I don't believe you've attended any religious services since moving to town. I know you don't attend mass. Does that make you a heathen?" It wasn't an accusation.

She tried to hide a smile. Father could ask the most personal questions and they never came across as impertinent. What a gift. She shook her head. "I prefer to think of myself as spiritual, not religious."

"Ah, I see." He nodded knowingly. "So whether the Gypsies are heathen or not is not for me to say. But this one couple and their two young children were genuinely interested in learning about the faith. Rohan and Martía Cooper. I met with them two or three times the week following their Sunday attendance. They had many questions and I did my best to answer them.

"Now Rohan was an excellent handyman, so I had him fix some odds and ends around the church. Performed minor miracles when it came to hammering and nailing. Martía, the mother, was an excellent cook and brought me enough food to last a month. She was also an excellent baker." Another twinkle. "In fact, she left me some recipe cards she'd hand copied. I didn't know what to do with them—I'm not much of a kitchen person myself—but she insisted I keep them just in case I got the urge to experiment."

"Which we did together when we used her spice cake recipe to make that wonderful Memory Cake." Dolly smiled at the recollection. But then she sighed. Although this trip down memory lane was fascinating, and the priest could indeed keep it interesting, she wasn't sure how relevant it was to Mack's urgent trip to the vet. Or why he gave the cat last rites. This was the most pressing question she had.

"You're wondering how this relates to Mack's illness," the priest inquired.

Dolly nodded, dumbly.

"Well, the family had a cat."

"You're not saying the Coopers gave you Mack...or Tozier, or whatever his name was at the time." As the priest nodded, she added, "That's just too unbelievable, Father. I'm sorry. Maybe they gave you a cat that looked like Mack?" The moment she said it, she regretted the implication. The poor priest had lost it.

Ignoring the remark, the elderly minister said, "No, the family didn't give me Mack."

Dolly was relieved.

"He simply stayed behind when they left a few weeks later."

Oh dear.

"But before they left, Martía gave me one more small care package. She must have realized that Mack wasn't going with them because in this basket were a few hand crafted pet toys, some kitty treats, and a small envelope of pills, like a prescription packet with instructions."

Without stopping to think how much of a believer her question made her sound, Dolly asked, "Well, what were the instructions?"

"Administer one pill to feline every twenty years."

She became an unbeliever again. "So I'm to believe that these pills extend Mack's life by twenty years. Father, do you realize how ridiculous this sounds?"

"I thought so at first as well. But Rohan and Martía were such a sincere couple. She told me Mack, Tozier, had been born eleven years before, in 1954, and in about nine years he'd get deathly sick. I was to give him his first dose then."

Dolly made a quick calculation. "So what happened in 1974?"

"By then Mack was well known around the church. He owned the building, it seemed. Now a few old timers complained about allowing a cat in the sanctuary, but most everyone else loved him, though he was as persnickety back then as he is today. Well, not *today*, perhaps, but you know what I mean."

She nodded. "Go on."

"One morning—forty years ago today, in fact—I unlocked the church and couldn't find him anywhere. I called, shook his treat bag, but he didn't come running. I found him near the altar. He was almost gone."

"Did you remember the pills?"

"To be honest, I'd completely forgotten about them. I wasn't a believer yet, you see."

"So what happened next?"

"I rushed him to the vet, like you did this morning. A Doctor Tobias had the practice back then. He put Mack on an IV but told me there wasn't much I could do. The cat was surely dying of old age, probably approaching the twenty year mark. When he said that, a light bulb went on and I rushed back here to the parish office and scrambled around until I found the envelope. There were eight pills inside."

Oh brother. Every time she got to the edge of her seat and caught up in the story, the old priest had to drop another outlandish detail and spoil the magic. Eight pills, eight more lives giving him a total of nine. Hmm. How original.

"Let me guess. You told Dr. Tobias to administer one dose in a last ditch effort to save Mack's life. What was the harm, he was going to die anyway, nothing to lose. But miraculously, Mack recovered. Fast forward twenty years to this same day, 1994, he gets sick again and you give him a second dose. Is that about the long and short of it?"

"I get the impression you don't believe me," the priest deadpanned.

"Well, you surely had me entertained with your storytelling skills, but no, I don't believe a word of it, Father. It sounds like a tale one might hear around a Gypsy campfire. Maybe to ease the pain of saying goodbye to a dearly beloved pet. A story to tell children to reassure them that their favorite dog or cat will live again. A metaphor, maybe, for the eternal nature of memories."

"I see you've been to college."

"You mean I've forgotten how to appreciate some of life's mysteries?" Maybe she had. She shook her head. "I'm just trying to wrap my brain around the fact that Mack is dying. If that's what you've been trying to help me see, then I appreciate your time and kind words. It's been very…interesting to say the least." Dolly rose to go. "Thank you for your time…."

*And for giving Mack his last rites.*

Father Aguilera rose as well. "One moment, I fear you've misunderstood my intent in telling you all this."

Dolly waited.

"There's more to this story than what I've shared. Would you care to hear the rest? We can walk in the garden, get some fresh air, clear our heads."

That was what she needed, yes. A clear head. "That would be lovely." She followed the elderly minister out of his office and into the sunlit courtyard directly behind the sanctuary of St. Anne's. It was a beautiful summer day, though a bit on the warm side for the high foothills that ramped up quickly to meet the majestic mountains of the Sierra Nevada range.

They strolled side by side enjoying the explosion of colorful roses and the aroma of freshly tilled soil and flowers. The priest continued his narrative. "Yes, Mack miraculously recovered in 1974 and lived another twenty years. But by 1994 he was back with Rohan and Martía and living in the Hut, though, of course, it wasn't called that then."

"So they must have returned. Are they the ones who turned the business into a small restaurant? The Log Cabin Café, I think it was called."

"Yes. And they stayed busy with the business until a few years ago."

Dolly knew this part of the story. The Coopers had to leave town for some unknown reason, but had left funds and instructions with the priest to pay any outstanding bills and, if they didn't return within a few months, to sell the building. They'd be well into their seventies, like Father Aguilera, she imagined. Maybe they moved to Florida and retired.

He continued. "When Mack almost died in '94 Martía asked me if I still had the envelope of pills. After what happened two decades before, you can bet I kept that prescription. I'd filed it safely away and returned it promptly when I heard our mutual friend was sick. Rohan and Martía never bothered with a vet, they healed him themselves. I saw Mack the next week when I dropped in for a cup of coffee. He was his old self." The priest chuckled at his unintended pun.

"Surely the cat was a different one. They brought another cat with them that looked like Mack. It was one of his own offspring, perhaps." She was full of explanations now. "And in 1974, that Dr. Tobias probably saw that you were heartbroken and…and exchanged cats somehow."

Father Aguilera gave Ma Tutt a withering glance. Similar to one Mack might have shot her after listening to her spout something utterly absurd.

But a sixty year old cat? Wasn't that utterly absurd? She didn't know where to go from there so she kept quiet trying to sort out her feelings. She wasn't frightened anymore. Sad, certainly, but no longer angry with the priest for visiting the vet. Suddenly, she remembered why she'd stormed over from Dr. Moore's office in the first place.

"Did you administer last rites to Mack this morning?"

The priest stopped walking and faced his guest. "Yes. I did administer the rite of extreme unction, and I'll tell you why. It's because…I no longer have the pills." A tear formed in his eye.

Pieces of the puzzle began to shift into place. "You don't have the prescription because you gave the envelope back to Martía, is that correct?" A nod. "And they never returned the envelope because Mack had returned to them." Another nod. "And Rohan and Martía owned the bakery before I did." She was confirming her suspicions.

"When they left a year and a half ago, Mack stayed behind. Again. He'd wander over to the parsonage and visit on occasion, but for the most part he hung around the Hut waiting, I suppose, for a new owner. For you."

Dolly was touched, but her mind was spinning. "Then that big cabinet *must* be theirs," she muttered to herself. "And all those recipe cards were definitely hers." More puzzle pieces. "Do you know if the Hut has a basement?" she asked abruptly.

"I'm not sure. I never inquired and the Coopers never mentioned it. But I'm not certain they would even if there was one. Why?"

It was Dolly's turn to tell a story, and she started with the discovery of the recipe card for those Irresistible Doughnuts. She told how everyone went crazy, overran her business, and what Mack did to save the day. The priest chuckled at the details and was glad he'd been on vacation when those events occurred. He would have hated acting the fool for participating in the rampage. Devouring anything edible and destroying the bakery! Oh my.

"So there is definitely something special about that cat." The priest readily agreed. Then she explained how the monstrous hutch had mysteriously moved about ten inches away from the wall to reveal a possible trap door.

The man of God said, "Yep, that sounds like Mack."

Dolly knew there was a story or two behind that remark, but tales of Mack's exploits would have to wait. "I think I know what's in the cellar," she said.

"I think you're right."

"The trouble is, that cabinet is just too heavy for

either one of us. Even together, we'd never budge it."

After a moment of contemplation, they both said in unison, "Big Ben!"

She'd only met him once, but Benjamin Reed was an original mountain man. He lived in a hand-hewn log cabin five miles up Shady Creek, one of many spring fed and snowmelt runoff streams that meandered down from the higher elevations. There was no road to his place, but a hearty soul could make the trek along a beaten path in about two hours.

Fortunately, neither Dolly nor Father Aguilera had to make the journey. Big Ben was in town to get supplies, the priest remembered. And he knew just where to find him. They beat their path to the local saloon.

"Um, should I go in and get him?" Dolly inquired. "I wouldn't want any of your parishioners to get the wrong impression if they see you enter such an establishment."

"And what kind of impression would that be, that priests don't drink? I think the Irish clergy dispelled that myth long ago, my dear."

Together they entered the old fashioned building, with swinging doors and a hitching post out front, *sans* horses. It wasn't really old fashioned, but tourists liked pretending they were entering a saloon straight from the gold rush era of the mid-1800s. It wasn't as dark and smoky as Dolly imagined it would be. This was California, after all, and smoking had been prohibited in public buildings for quite a few years. Still, the place did exude that rustic tavern feel.

They looked around and the priest nodded to the bar. Sitting at the last barstool, hunkered a bear-sized patron downing the last drop of ale from a frosty mug. He wiped his mouth with the back of his hand and said in a loud but friendly voice, "Dex, I'm still thirsty!"

"Coming right up," replied the barkeep, another burly man who, though not as tall and thick as Big Ben, matched him when it came to the length and thickness of his beard.

Ben caught the two visitors looking at him. He smiled and waved them over.

"Ma Tutt! What are you doing in here? Hello, Reverend! Can I order you your usual?"

Father Aguilera caught Dolly feigning shock and returned an embarrassed grimace. "Not today, son. We're on a mission."

"We need your muscles," Ma Tutt added boldly.

"You picked the right man. Need another tree lifted off a car?"

The parish priest shook his head. During a storm last winter, one of the many California Oaks surrounding the church had fallen across a parishioner's vehicle during morning mass. Fortunately, no one was injured, but until Big Ben had come along the parking lot was blocked and no one could get home for lunch.

"Not quite as dramatic as your Paul Bunyan feat in January, but we sure can't do it alone."

"Just need a piece of furniture scooted a few feet

is all," Dolly assured him. "I can pay in doughnuts."

"Well, let's hop to it! Dex, skip my refill." Ben slapped some money on the counter.

"But I already poured it!" the bartender said, looking sadly at his sixteen ounce creation with a perfect head of foam.

Ben slapped some more money down. "Then I'll pay it forward. Surprise your next lucky customer."

"That would be me," Dex said as he took a long draw on the mug of cold beer. "Thanks, Ben."

Everyone laughed.

The three of them made their way up Main Street to the Hut; the California sun beat warmly upon their backs. A steady flow of cars streamed by, mostly filled with families heading for a quick weekend escape from the haze of the valley. It was Saturday afternoon and that darned Creamy Pie—the competition!—was doing a fair business. The smell of grease and fried dough hung heavy in the air.

"You should stay open later, Ma. Look at all the traffic you're missing. See there? A young couple's peeking in your front window wondering why the lights are off." Big Ben pointed and sure enough, a man and woman dressed in odd billowy garb and colorful scarves hanging from their waists were standing at the front door of Ma Tutt's Donut Hut.

They were just about to turn and leave when Father Aguilera cried out, "Rohan! Martía! Welcome back!"

Dolly gawked. Surely not. This couple was *young*!

The old friends embraced and laughed and exchanged *Great to see yous*! Then introductions were made. Dolly couldn't believe it. Big Ben simply smiled in recognition, a toothy grin spread across his face. "I remember you folks from a few years ago. Owned this here café before Ma came to town."

Rohan, a slim man with a dark complexion, dark hair, and bushy eyebrows said, "We're just passing through and we wanted to drop in and say hello to Tozier. Tomorrow's his birthday, you know." He had a trace of an accent, something vaguely European. Dolly couldn't place it, but was mesmerized by the gentle lilt of his voice. When Martía spoke, she was entranced.

"We've been traveling so much, Father, we lost track of days. When we realized our mistake, we had to hurry to get here. He'll need his next dose of *fenexia* very soon now."

"Fenexia? Is that Mack's annual prescription that he needs to take every…twenty years?" Dolly delivered her line with a chuckle and a poke of her elbow. The others looked at her with blank stares. Her smile quickly faded. "Ahem. Well, it's not that I don't believe you…"

"You don't believe us," Father Aguilera said.

"Okay, you're right. But I'd do anything to try to help Mack. He's at Dr. Moore's right now, and he's not doing well." They all exchanged worried looks.

"Martía, do you know where his pills are?" Ma Tutt was already unlocking the bakery and leading them inside.

"I think we left them in the cellar," the Gypsy woman explained. "We had to leave town rather quickly. When that sneaky devil was appointed Inspector General and started poking around, we couldn't risk staying any longer."

This bit of information brought Dolly up short. Another mystery. "By sneaky devil, do you mean Donovan Huckly?"

"He's the one," Rohan said. "Took it upon himself to, how do you say, stick his nostrils into our business."

"He's up to something, that's for certain," agreed Dolly, not bothering to correct the misspoken idiom. "I didn't even know the Hut had a basement until he came by this morning wanting to inspect it. Said he had to make sure the foundation was solid. I don't trust him. He wants something down there."

"Did he find it?" Martía wanted to know.

"No, but I discovered something strange while he was here." She then explained where she'd found Mack early that morning and how she'd realized later that the cabinet had somehow moved to reveal a latch in the floorboards. "And that's why Big Ben is here. He's going to help us move the hutch so we can open that door."

Everyone agreed it was a good plan. They huddled around the big wooden kitchen cupboard like a football team. Dolly was the quarterback and called the plays. They broke and Big Ben wedged himself as best he could between the cabinet and the wall so he could simply push the piece of furniture further along its path and clear the way to the door in the floor. Rohan would have the honors of opening the trap door and Martía would lead the crew down into the mystery cellar. "Father, I guess you can pray."

The plan went off without a hitch and soon they were all in the basement, except for Big Ben Reed who feared he'd get stuck down there. Rohan flipped a switch and the place illuminated quite nicely. It was as cool as a cave and looked like one too, having been carved out of the mountain back in '38. Dolly quickly scanned for bats and was relieved to find nothing more than a few cobwebs in the corners of the quite spacious underground room.

She stood amazed at the overflowing shelves. The whole basement was chockfull of canned goods, supplies, more recipe cards and books, and rows and rows of exotic spices—none of which she'd heard of when she quickly scanned their labels. Reviewing the glass jars of canned fruit and vegetables, she said, "You could feed an army!"

"Yes," Martía said. "We have at least a year's supply of food here. In case of a zombie apocalypse."

Dolly shot her a glance, but the woman seemed dead serious. Though with Gypsies, you never knew. Father Aguilera simply chuckled.

"Well, first things first. Do you know where you put the felixia?" But Martía was already shuffling through some shelves like a bloodhound on a trail.

"I think we're looking for fenexia. Felix is a cartoon cat, my dear." The priest had that twinkle in his eye again.

"Oh, all right, Father Funny."

"Found it," Martía exclaimed.

Just then Big Ben called from up above. "We have a visitor."

"Tell them we're closed. We open bright and early tomorrow at five."

"Oh, I'm busy tomorrow," called a familiar voice. "So if you don't mind, I'll simply come down and inspect your basement right now. Shouldn't take too long."

Above them, the face of Donovan Huckly appeared. Dolly could see he was wearing his steel gray work shirt. Building Code and Zoning.

"What about your mama bear and her cubs?" she called back up, not that she was interested.

As Donovan scrambled down the drop ladder steps he said, "Helped them move along up the mountain by banging a of couple pots together. Took less time than I thought."

Wonderful.

In no time, Huckly was standing among them, looking around with wide eyes while everyone stared at him with the same. He finally realized who made up his audience. "Well, if it isn't the Coopers. I see you haven't changed a bit. And I see we do have a basement after all." He pointed at the walls as if they were hidden from view. "Won't take but a few minutes to determine the structural integrity of this building." And with that, he navigated around the room, poking here and there at the walls with some kind of metal instrument. Every now and then he'd emit some guttural comments while the others looked on in silence. "Uh huh. Uh huh. Ohhh. Ah hah!"

It was but a few minutes later, though to Ma it seemed like an eternity, when Donovan pronounced his verdict. "I'm afraid I have some bad news."

"Let me guess," Dolly said. "You're going to have to condemn the building."

"Oh, nothing so drastic. But I will have to shut your business down until I make a full inspection. Seems there's some crumbling at the corners. Some water damage. Might have a hidden spring behind this part of the mountain that might cause some leakage if we don't get on it right away. It'll take a few weeks to do a full assessment."

"A few weeks? Can't you tell me now what needs to be done and I'll call some contractors and start making repairs on Monday." To Dolly's untrained eye, there didn't appear to be any damage whatsoever. She would certainly get a second opinion before committing to spending any money.

"I'm afraid not. I'll need full access to the building. Starting immediately."

"This is ridiculous! You can't just…"

Father Aguilera raised his hand calmly and Dolly's rising rant subsided. He gently took Donovan's elbow and led him away from the others. After a quiet conversation, they returned to the group.

"Seems there's been a slight misunderstanding," Donovan began. "I'll be back Monday with my supervisor who will make a full inspection. It will be determined at that point whether we'll need to close your business or not. Good day." The Inspector General abruptly worked his way up the ladder and left.

"What do you have on him?" Dolly wondered aloud. The priest's eyes merely glimmered. "Well, whatever it is, we have the rest of the weekend to sort it all out. Something about this basement intrigues that man, and I aim to discover the mystery before he does." She considered the Gypsy couple. "Unless you know something you aren't telling us."

"Oh, there is always something that wants for an explanation," Martía replied cryptically. She waved the small envelope yellowed with age. "But many times, the answer, once discovered, is unsatisfying...to the unbelieving mind."

Dolly let that sink in for a moment. "Well, I don't know whether my mind believes or not, but I do know Mack is sick. And if this pill can help him, then we need to hurry. Last time I saw Doc Moore, he said it didn't look good."

"Yes," Martía said. "Time is critical. For tomorrow is his birthday."

Dolly wondered about this second mention of Mack's birthday. The day seemed very significant to the Gypsy couple. With a renewed sense of urgency, the four of them scrambled up the ladder and joined Big Ben, ready to save the life of their feline friend.

Doctor Gerald Moore met the crew as they entered the small reception area. His face was grave and he shook his head slightly when his eyes met Dolly's. She and Martía followed him to the exam room while the men waited in awkward silence, as useless as snow chains in summer.

Despite the mood, Martía let out a joyful greeting when she saw her old friend. Mack managed to rally and raised his head. A pathetic mew escaped his throat before he laid his head back down on the exam table. The IV line was connected to his front paw and wrapped in fluorescent green tape. On his other leg was his name tag with his weight, sex, and approximate age of eighteen. Dolly tittered nervously when she saw it. "I think he's twenty," she said. "Tomorrow, in fact."

"Oh?"

"Well, according to her former owner, if cats have owners, that is." She introduced Martía.

"I remember you now," Doc Moore said. "You and your husband had the Log Cabin Café at the north end of town, is that right?"

"That is correct. We had to leave unexpectedly two years ago, but Toz...er, Mack, decided to stay. We are so happy that Dolly has taken such a liking to him."

"She has indeed. She rushed him here this morning..." He paused uncomfortably. "I hesitate to say it, but I'm afraid at twenty years of age, his time is just about up." The cat's breathing was labored and his eyes were glazing over.

Martía nodded her head in understanding. "Would you mind, then, if Dolly and I spent some time alone with him? To say our goodbyes and all."

"By all means." Gerry closed the door behind him and went to chat with the men waiting at the front of the clinic.

Dolly raised an eyebrow. "To say our goodbyes?"

"Well. A goodbye to one lifetime at least."

"How do you mean?"

Martía produced the prescription packet. "This will be his third pill," she said by way of explanation. "He's ready to start his fourth life. Out of nine, of course."

Of course. "So you actually believe each pill gives Mack another twenty years of life?" Dolly thought for a moment. "What was the name of this drug again?"

"Fenexia," Martía said with a slight accent.

"You mean…Phoenixia. As in…the Phoenix. Like, the rise of?"

With a sly smile, Martía gave one dose to Mack, who barely had the strength to open his mouth to receive it. Fortunately, unlike other domestic longhairs, Mack knew what to do with the pill and managed to swallow it. He shut his eyes, his breathing slowed. In a few moments it ceased altogether.

Dolly grabbed Martía's hand in alarm.

"It's time for us to go. Goodbye my friend." The Gypsy woman ran her free hand over the matted fur of her longtime companion. Then she turned to leave.

"What? No. Wait." Dolly couldn't take her eyes off the still form lying silent on the table.

"Trust in God," was all the Gypsy said as she led her new friend out of the room.

Back in the front office, Rohan looked up in anticipation and received a gentle smile from his wife. "He's at peace. Doctor, would you allow my husband to carry him home with us?"

Gerry said that would be fine and went to confirm that Mack had died. After a few moments, he brought the limp body to them, wrapped in the apron Ma Tutt had used to carry him in that very morning. Tears flowed down her face. Even Big Ben wiped at his eyes.

They walked back to the Hut in silence.

It was all too confusing. Father Aguilera with his strange tale, the timely appearance of Rohan and Martía, the pills, the promise. But now the reality. Mack was dead. Who were these people, after all? She didn't know them. Why should she trust them? Even the priest had become a stranger to her. Dolly stopped in her tracks.

"What are we doing? Where are we going?" She was lost. The sun was setting.

Martía hugged her. "Rohan will bury Mack up the hill a ways, behind the café. Then, we go home, we say our prayers, we go to bed." She let go and held Dolly's shoulders, her dark eyes penetrating to the soul of the woman in front of her. "Let's see what the new dawn brings, shall we?"

Dolly let herself be led into the bakery. The three of them sat at a table while Rohan left by the back door with the bundle that was Mack. She looked at the naked shelves. The place was as empty as the hollow in her heart. She had nothing prepared for the next morning and no energy to whip up even a tray of treats. But then, tomorrow was Sunday and she still hadn't decided if she wanted to be open seven days a week. Well, if she lost one day's customers to Creamy Pie, then so be it. She'd beat them up again starting Monday…but she doubted even by then that her heart would be in it.

When Rohan returned Dolly cried.

Dolores Tutt hadn't been to church for nearly twenty years. If she were to start back up, the last option would be a Catholic church. There were just too many foreign aspects to the service. When to stand up and when to kneel. When to bow and when to respond aloud. And she'd never crossed herself in her life, except when she played a nun in a high school play, but even then she thought she'd done it wrong.

Nevertheless, at ten o'clock Sunday morning she found herself in a pew beside Rohan and Martía. They greeted her warmly with hugs and smiles and scooched over so she could sit at the aisle in case she decided to bolt. After some initial trepidation, however, she found herself at peace as the pipe organ played and the choir sang and the readers quoted from sacred texts. The incense, like the people's prayers it symbolized, drifted heavenward.

When Father Emilio Aguilera got up to speak, she was ready to listen. It was a short homily, nothing too profound or original, but the topic of hope in the midst of life's difficulties was one that touched her heart. It sort of reminded her of a cream filled Danish. Tasty and satisfying for the moment, but nothing too substantial for the long term. Or so she thought. Her evaluation was to be expected; she was not yet a believer.

The four of them met after the service once the priest had greeted all the congregants. Big Ben had returned to his mountain cabin the night before, but promised to check in on Dolly in a week or so. It was a nice gesture, seeing as how he didn't really know Mack. He did know the cat had meant a lot to her, though.

"Let's go to the Hut and I can put on some coffee. I have to get ready for tomorrow anyway. The doughnuts won't magically appear." She grimaced at her inadvertent turn of phrase.

"You never know!" Martía's laugh was like a wind chime, bright and cheery.

"Well, at least one of us is in a good mood." Ma sighed.

The interior of the Hut was darkened, of course, but enough light penetrated through the plate glass windows to reveal that all was as it should be. Tables were clear, chairs were positioned correctly, the display case was empty. *Whew!* She couldn't handle that kind of miracle right now despite María's half-believable jest.

She unlocked the front door and the small party made their way inside.

Part of her brain was expecting a feline greeting and as she turned on the lights she thought she heard a guttural yowl. But as she stopped to listen, there was only the grinding hum of the ice machine. She wiped away an escaping tear.

"Make yourselves at home. I'll start the coffee," she managed to say without her voice cracking.

And then a bang from the back room.

Putting aside the foil packets, Dolly led her small troupe into the kitchen and they stared at the open back door. Someone must have broken in during the night. Maybe someone was still inside. She grabbed a kitchen knife.

Rohan quickly checked the walk-in storage room. Nothing had been disturbed. Another noise. This time from the basement. They gathered around the trap door next to the hutch. She gave Rohan a nod and he yanked at the latch in the flooring, revealing the entrance to the cave-like cellar.

"Come on out of there, you rascally devil," he said, but his tone was teasing and his mirth transparent.

Mack bounded out of the basement and greeted them with a loud series of meows, chirrups, and throaty scoldings. He was hungry and no one had fed him!

Dolly dropped the knife. Her hand covered her mouth.

Then she ran and scooped up the gray mackerel, turning him over unceremoniously to examine him for familiar markings. The white patch on the belly. The v-shaped scar on his right ear. The pronounced M on his forehead that went half way down his nose. They were all there! This was Mack. This couldn't be Mack. This had to be Mack. She spun him around and around, dancing with him as if he were her high school beau at a Sadie Hawkins dance. He was yowling in protest.

Soon everyone was joining in the celebration. There were hugs and kisses and pats on the back as if they were somehow responsible for the miracle before them. While they laughed, Mack squirmed his way out of their grasp and dashed under the counter, refusing to be coaxed back into the wonderful melee.

Martía took the liberty to whip up a little something to eat and Father Aguilera found the cat food and filled Mack's dish. The tabby hesitated long enough to make sure even the priest wouldn't pursue him and began his late breakfast, anxiously glancing over his shoulder after every bite.

They returned to the dining room and Dolly collapsed into a chair. She simply shook her head for a good couple of minutes. In no time, coffee and cookies were distributed, appearing like loaves and fishes at the feeding of the five thousand. Mack eventually made his way to the four-top and jumped to the center of the table, taking his rightful spot as the center of attention. He began his after breakfast bath.

"Well, you made quite the grand entrance, mister!" Ma said. "The kitty door not good enough for you anymore?"

Mack licked his paw and swiped his ear, keeping mum for now as to why the back door was open and what he was doing in the basement. Dolly just shook her head some more. A cat's reasons for doing anything are inscrutable anyway.

"So if I'm not mistaken, Father," she said, including Rohan and Martía in her conversation, "Mack turned sixty…today." The three of them shrugged and nodded as if this kind of thing happened every day.

She focused again on the tabby, petting him to assure herself he was real. "Well, that makes us the same age, dear kitty. You're starting over and so am I." She glanced about the Hut and smiled at the priest and her two new friends. "In a sense, I've already begun a new life this year."

"Here's to many more," Martía said. Rohan and Father Aguilera raised their coffee mugs.

Dolly thought about her early retirement from a boring corporate job in the valley and how Ma Tutt's

Donut Hut had given her a renewed sense of purpose. She accepted the toast and raised her mug as well. "To the future."

"Here here," came the response.

Mack *mreowed* in agreement and sidled up for a back rub.

"Sixty!" she said again.

And this time she almost believed it.

## 'Tail' Number Four
## Forgettable Pie

Monday morning was a blur. The Hut was busy with its steady stream of customers, but more importantly Mack, her gray mackerel, was back and looking sleek and healthy, just as a young cat should. Young? According to her new friends, Rohan and Martía Cooper, Mack was now sixty years old!

Dolly still couldn't quite believe it. The emotional events of the past few days threatened to overwhelm her, but her eyes couldn't be wrong. Mack had died at Doc Moore's office and now he was alive! Father Aguilera assured her it was true. He'd celebrated Mack's 'rebirthday' twenty years before... and twenty years before that. He was beginning his fourth of nine lives.

She had to ask Martía about the prescription that had given Mack this second, er fourth, chance at life. *Fenexia*. If such a pill could do that for cats....

Dolly shook her head, not wanting to go there.

And yet….

The door to the Hut jingled shut and the last customer of the morning left with a "See you tomorrow, Ma!" Dolly waved goodbye, exhausted but happy. It was just past noon and the till was full. Plus, there had been no sign of Donovan Huckly, the nosey city code inspector who'd threatened to drop in today and shut down her doughnut shop. Well, the day was only half over; but she was not in the mood for any more surprises.

"Would you mind locking the door, Rohan?" Ma Tutt asked. "And flipping the sign? We sold out again, which is fantastic, but it's time to clean up and get ready for tomorrow." Martía came out from the kitchen and began wiping down the tables. Rohan did as requested then picked up a broom and started sweeping the floors. "I want to thank you both again for all you've done—and all you're doing!—to help out."

"*Oosh*, it is nothing," Rohan said with a dismissive wave of a hand.

"Now, it's quite a bit more than nothing," Dolly replied. "Healing Mack, if that's the right word, and agreeing to stick around a few weeks has really set my mind at ease."

After celebrating Mack's return the day before, Dolly had started worrying. They'd come from church yesterday only to discover the back door of the bakery had been busted wide open. Someone had forced the lock and broken in, that much was obvious. Her suspicions fell on Donovan, but she had no hard evidence to prove anything. Rohan, a wizard with tools, had easily fixed the lock and secured the back entrance. Nothing seemed to have been stolen, but the break in had Ma concerned, so the Coopers agreed to help out until everything returned to normal.

As if hosting a miracle cat and baking with magical spices could ever be considered normal.

Then there was the fact that they themselves were not quite normal. The Coopers were a Gypsy couple who'd owned the small café before Dolly had bought it and turned it into Ma Tutt's Donut Hut. But Dolly wasn't thinking of their strange attire or their faintly European accent that hinted at their unique ethnicity. She was wondering about their age.

They were young!

But according to the elderly priest, he'd known them since 1965 when they first arrived in the small mountain community of Sugar Pine Station. They were part of a Gypsy band that was traveling through the area when Father Aguilera had met them. They had two young children with them at the time, but evidently the son and daughter had grown up like all children do. Grown *older* like all people do.

All people, except Martía and Rohan. Evidently, they hadn't aged since the 1960s!

Ma wondered if they'd been taking *fenexia* as well.

"We need to talk," she said at last. The Hut was

sparkling, the kitchen prepped for an early morning start. The priest was back at his parish office and Mack had finished lunch and was bedding down for an early afternoon nap in the sun. It was just the three of them and it was time to lay all the cards on the table.

But where to begin? She had so many questions. And doubts. She wanted to believe that somehow some mysterious, mystical world was breaking into her own, but she couldn't just jump blindly into it, could she? Surely there were answers that would ease her way, maybe not complete explanations but clues that made some kind of sense once they were lined up.

So far these clues simply led to a host of new questions. Like, is Mack truly magical and does every two-decade dose of *fenexia* actually give him another life? And what about the Gypsy couple's long lifespan and their apparent youthfulness? Then, not least and probably not last, what is Donovan's role in all of this? Why the obsessive interest in her basement and is there some kind of connection between them all? These were the big questions Dolly had and she was sure there were more to come.

They gathered around a four-top in the dining area and Ma folded her hands nervously. "I'm not quite sure how to begin, so I'll just start with a few main ingredients and we can add to them as we go." She'd learned long ago that baking was a good metaphor for all kinds of life situations.

The Coopers glanced at each other and nodded. "We have nothing to hide from you," Rohan said. "Tozier trusts you and so do we," added Martía. "Just like with Father Aguilera."

Tozier was Mack's original name and she'd get to his story eventually, but the mention of the kindly priest and their relationship with him seemed like as good a starting point as any.

"Well, I'm pleased and flattered, to be sure. I feel I can also trust Father Aguilera. So let's begin there. Have you really known him for almost fifty years?"

"Yes," Martía said, commencing the narrative while Rohan, content to listen, sat quietly. "In the summer of 1965, our small Romany clan camped at what is now the recreational park south of town. We stayed for a month or so, working odd jobs, selling baked goods and trinkets, earning a little money before moving north toward Oregon. For many years our band traveled up and down the west coast, from Baja California to Alaska, never staying longer than six months in any location."

"Then what made you two want to settle down in Sugar Pine Station? If I have my math right, you owned the Log Cabin Café for almost eighteen years before you left in 2012 or so. Is that about right?"

"Yes, we opened the restaurant in early 1994. But we actually built the log cabin back in 1938 on our first visit."

If Dolly had been drinking coffee she would have spewed it across the table top.

"What? You can't be serious. That would make you..." She tried to calculate.

"We're both one hundred years of age," Rohan said, saving her the trouble.

She stared at them in silence. Looking hard for any facial wrinkles or age spots or gray hair, Dolly finally shook her head. Her mouth was dry. She needed something to drink. Holding a finger up to pause the conversation, she got up and put a tea kettle on to boil. She sat back down, gathered her scattered thoughts and said, "Okay, help me understand...you lived in Sugar Pine Station in the 1930s?" More doubts, but maybe the story would unfold in a way that would eventually make sense.

"No," Martía contradicted gently. "Our clan was simply passing from one place to another, as our people have done for generations. We stopped here briefly; the community back then no more than a cluster of homes and stores on a mountain road. We were twenty-four and newly married; Rohan already a master carpenter, so good with his hands. A businessman hired him to construct a building, a store for selling supplies to fishermen and hunters on their way to Yosemite."

"Yes, a bait and tackle shop."

The tea kettle whistled and Ma started to get up. Rohan motioned for her to remain seated and went to prepare three cups. Martía continued. "When digging the basement, Rohan had to cut away at some of the rock. This building practically fits right up against the mountainside as it is, so going down meant breaking part way into the granite layer below the surface. I was helping him clear the rubble when a section of rock gave way. A thin ribbon of water trickled out from a crack."

"That's not a good sign if you're digging a basement."

"You're right. We showed it to the owner who asked if Rohan could plug it up. He said it might be possible with tar pitch and a few rock fragments. He didn't know how long the patch would last, however, but the man said for us to go ahead. So he stopped the flow of water."

"But not before we had some tea from that tiny spring." Rohan brought three cups of hot water to the table and set them down. He placed a selection of flavored teas before them along with a plate of cookies. "I found these leftovers from yesterday's celebration. Hope you don't mind."

Dolly ignored the treats but opened a tea pouch mindlessly, then set the teabag to seep. "You drank from the spring?"

"It was pure and sweet," Martía explained, "without the taste of minerals, so we filled a teapot and brewed a mix of black tea leaves and herbs. I've wished ever since that I'd written down what ingredients I'd used." The Gypsy woman grew quiet and looked knowingly at her husband who smiled in sympathy.

"Why?" Dolly asked, but even as she asked it,

she suspected she knew the answer. "You stopped aging after that, didn't you?"

Both her guests nodded.

"Was it the water? Or was it the leaves?" Ma pulled the teabag out of her cup, looked at it as if it might contain arsenic, then put it back in to seep some more.

"A combination, we think," Rohan answered. "For the owner tasted the water but didn't join us for tea. And he's long since passed."

"And the herbal leaves came from a friend, who has also passed." A moment. "A few years later I started writing down all of my recipes. I began experimenting with various herbs, spices, exotic ingredients. I sought out the old recipes that had been handed down by word of mouth, recording them, preserving them. I knew…."

"You knew something had changed." Dolly brought the cup to her lips, hesitated, then took a tentative sip.

"…I knew we had to find a cure."

"A cure? For what, eternal youth? Why?" She looked at the couple skeptically.

Rohan answered that concern. "Within ten years we were certain something was wrong. Our friends and cousins said we looked as young as we did on our wedding day. It was not a compliment. We caught them staring, overheard them whispering. They were withdrawing from us, shunning us."

"So we left." Martía's cup of hot water sat

untouched, cooling. "We wandered the countryside, just the two of us, eventually joining another group of Romany working the grape and raisin harvests in the Central Valley."

Dolly sat up straight at this, but didn't interrupt. She remembered a Gypsy band staying on her parents' farm south of Fresno when she was a young girl. She wondered if she'd met this couple way back when.

Mr. Cooper said, "We settled in with our new extended family. We had two children of our own. We adopted Tozier." He smiled and looked at Mack. At the sound of his name, the gray tabby got up and stretched. He moved from one soft chair by the window to the next, catching up with the sunbeam's new location, then settled down to continue his nap. Within moments he was purring loudly.

"And in 1965, you, your children, and Mack visited Sugar Pine Station again," Dolly surmised. "That's when you met Father Aguilera."

"He is such a kind man," Martía said. "We didn't exactly explain what had happened to us, but we had questions, you see. Questions about our…condition. Questions about eternal life."

"The Father answered our concerns with much grace and patience," Rohan added. "He spoke to us of eternity and, though we still had questions, we believed. Even Tozier—Mack here—trusted the gentle priest."

"And before you left, Martía, when you realized

that Mack was going to stay behind, did he believe *you* when you spoke to him about the medicine? The *fenexia*?"

"Not at first, no. But when Tozier died nine years later, I think he must have believed. He evidently gave our friend the required dose, for here he is." She indicated the sleeping cat.

Mack lazily rolled over on his back and stretched himself lengthwise on the overstuffed chair, completely relaxed, in heaven. Dolly couldn't resist the temptation. She got up and scratched the mackerel's belly. He responded by revving his purr motor. Rohan laughed quietly.

Certain clues were starting to make sense. The Coopers had stumbled upon an elixir, an herbal concoction that when brewed with a mountain spring, probably special in its own right, created a kind of fountain of youth.

"So you're not taking *fenexia*?" she asked.

Martía laughed. "No, it's an old Romany remedy for old age—effective in felines only! Sadly, it does not prevent a cat from dying by other means. They aren't immortal, you know."

"You mean cats don't *magically* have nine lives?" Dolly asked, sincerely. The two stared at her as if she were off her rocker. "Well, you have to admit, sometimes strange things do occur when Mack's around. He's…kind of special, wouldn't you say?" She patted his belly once more before returning to her tea, now cold.

"Mack is definitely special, in more ways than one. An odd side effect of the *fenexia*, we think. But this ancient remedy for feline aging did prompt us to test other spices and compounds for different side effects. I've been experimenting for over sixty years and have created a number of recipes, some of which have produced strange and curious results."

"Like your Irresistible Doughnuts and your scrumptious Memory Cake?"

"Ah, I see you found some of my recipe cards," Martía said, pleased. "Yes. Nature has yet to reveal all her secrets. But we'll keep searching. If one ingredient can bring back a cat's youth, then surely another can start the aging process again."

Why this Gypsy couple wanted to start aging was beyond Dolly. Think of it! Eternally young. Eternally healthy. You could explore the world; experience all that life has to offer. Sure, you'd probably have to move every ten years or so if you didn't want to raise suspicions. And you'd have to leave your friends. And your family. You'd watch your children grow older, of course. See them age…and die.

"What happened to your children?" Dolly asked, suddenly.

"They grew up, healthy and strong, and have remained with our adopted clan to this day. When they were old enough to manage on their own, we left, fearful that our condition would once again cause fear and anger." Martía grew silent, then whispered, "We never told them why we had to leave, which has

115

been the most painful part of our story. And we haven't seen them, except from a distance, since." She began to sob quietly while Rohan held her close.

After a moment, he continued their saga. "We traveled on our own once more, wandering from here to there until we decided to return to Sugar Pine Station to celebrate Tozier's fortieth birthday. We guessed that few, if any of the town's residents, would remember us from thirty years before."

"Other than Father Aguilera," Dolly said.

"Yes. He had Tozier's prescription, you see, so we had to visit him. He was obviously surprised but very pleased, and was not afraid. We told him about building the log cabin…the spring, the tea. We told him everything. He never doubted. He said God knew the path laid out before us and would never leave us. But most of all, he was just so happy to see us, and when he asked us to stay, we couldn't refuse. So we bought this building, opened the Log Cabin Café, and settled in for almost twenty years."

"It was a wonderful time," Martía said, "but we stayed too long." Rohan agreed with a sigh and a cluck of his tongue.

"Because Donovan started poking around," Dolly said, suddenly connecting the dots. "Do you think he suspects something? Do you think he knows that you…haven't aged?"

"He suspects," Rohan said. "He knows we have a secret, though we aren't exactly sure of his thoughts. Nevertheless, he threatened to expose us."

"But how? Why?" Ma exclaimed. "What does he hope to gain?"

Before they could answer, their conversation was interrupted by the movement of an approaching figure outside, striding purposely across the street. He stopped at the front door of the Hut. The windows of the café were slightly tinted so it wasn't immediately obvious to someone passing by whether anyone was inside or not. The three of them watched as the man hesitated briefly before cupping his hands along the side of his face and peered in.

Thomas J. Fairbanks, editor of the *Sugar Pine Station Bulletin*, pulled back from the glass when he saw three pairs of eyes staring back at him. He rapped his knuckles on the glass door. Dolly let out an exasperated sigh. "Why have a Closed sign? Seems like no one bothers to read it!" At least it wasn't Donovan, she thought.

Ma gave an apologetic shrug to her guests and opened the door. She hadn't seen the newspaper man since the Irresistible Doughnut disaster. Oh, and once in a nightmare she had a few weeks afterward. She really hadn't given him much thought since then, to be honest, but now that he was standing there, dressed semi-business casual, she was struck at how handsome he was. Mid-sixties, probably, but fit, trim, and tan, with just the right amount of gray in his closely cropped brown hair.

What was she thinking? He'd almost attacked her like a zombie in *Shaun of the Dead*!

"What can I do for you, Mr. Fairbanks." She wasn't going to invite him in just yet.

"Oh, please, call me Tommy." He stood there awkwardly. "Um, do you mind if I come in? I won't stay but a minute."

Reluctantly, she stepped aside and invited him to sit at the table with the Coopers. He looked at the plate of cookies and remarked, "Those look very good."

Ma grunted. "Help yourself. Would you care for some hot tea?" She was going through the motions of being polite, but just wasn't feeling it at the moment.

"That would be delightful," Tommy said, oblivious to the chilly reception. "But only if it's no trouble." He gave her a wink. Was he flirting?

"Not at all," Rohan said after an awkward pause in which the hostess did nothing. He went to attend to the tea kettle.

Tommy didn't wait for the hot water before grabbing a cookie and taking a bite. "Mmm," was all he had to say this time. Dolly looked on, her patience wearing thin.

"Again, Mr. Fairbanks...um, Tommy, what can I do for you?"

He swallowed and said, "I actually dropped by so that I might do something for you. But first, I...I have to apologize for my actions from a number of weeks back. I, along with other upstanding members of our community, destroyed your shop and I failed to return to join in the cleanup. I...I was embar-

rassed, you see. But I felt I had to make things right.
I'm sorry it's taken me so long to tell you."

"Water under the bridge," Dolly said, warming at
his apology. "At least you didn't print anything about
it in the weekly *Bulletin*." When she saw Martía's
questioning look, she added, "Long story."

Rohan brought fresh cups of hot water for
everyone. As they all set their teabags to seep and
nibbled on cookies, Dolly glanced at the pair of
overstuffed chairs, wondering if Mack wanted an
afternoon treat as well. He wasn't there. Evidently,
he'd slipped away when Tommy showed up. Not
surprising, given his general disdain for strangers.

Tommy was saying, "Of course not, but I would
like to feature the Hut in an upcoming edition. Maybe
take the angle of running a successful business in the
shadow of a popular doughnut franchise." He
indicated the place across the street with a toss of his
head.

Creamy Pie! Dolly fumed. The homogenization
of America was what it was. Small towns losing their
quaint little charm; architecturally unique, if
sometimes odd and curious, buildings giving way to
big box stores and generic storefronts. Pretty soon,
every city across the country would blur into one
bland mess of retail malls, boring restaurants, and
office buildings.

"I'll think about it," she said. "Is that what you
had in mind, when you said you could do something
for me?"

"Not quite, but I certainly don't mind promoting a local business in the paper. Actually, I have something to show you." He looked at Rohan and Martía intently. "I think you both will be interested in this as well." Tommy reached into his back pocket and brought out a copy of a newspaper clipping and photograph. He unfolded it, straightening the creases. Then he turned it around, laying it flat on the table for the others to read. It was dated 1965.

Dolly voiced the headline: "Gypsy Troupe in Sugar Pine Station." The caption to the photograph read: "Company of Romany Offer Goods & Services." The picture featured an enclosed wagon decked out like a traveling medicine show. There were pots and pans hanging from hooks, an assortment of tools and toys scattered about, and disorderly shelves of jars and bottles and such. Standing beside the display, with laughter on their lips, was a young Gypsy family.

Martía gasped. Rohan sucked in his breath. Dolly said, "Oh my lands."

"So it's true," Tommy said, sitting back in amazement. "This is you, isn't it? You're the young couple. Not the children all grown up? No, you couldn't be the children anyway. They'd be in their late fifties by now. Huckly was right."

At the mention of Donovan Huckly, Ma Tutt sputtered, "What in the world do you mean by that?" She turned to the young—*no, old!*—couple for answers, for any hint as to what this all meant.

Rohan met her questioning gaze. He placed a finger on the piece of paper and pointed. "It is true, this is me, Martía, and our children, Rebecca and Hadriel."

"He promised he wouldn't show this to anyone if we left," Martía said, glaring at the newspaper editor. Tommy raised his hand as if warding off an evil spirit.

"Wait, what?" Dolly asked. "You've seen this picture before?"

"Yes," Rohan said. "Two years ago, this Mr. Huckly showed us the picture, so full of himself, convinced we were hiding some deep, dark secret. We tried to deny it was us, but he said he'd expose us 'to the world' if we didn't pack up and leave immediately."

"He was very dramatic, yes, but I think it was more from fear than anything else," Martía said. "He suspected something unusual had happened to us, but was nervous all the same. Maybe that's why he wanted us to leave."

"That could be," Tommy said, "but his trepidation hasn't stopped him from trying to figure out the mystery surrounding your apparent lack of aging. He's on to something and has stepped up his game these past few months."

"I can attest to that," Ma added. "He's been trying to shut down the Hut ever since I opened in May. I think he's searching for something. He might have even broken in the other night, but I can't prove anything."

Tommy shook his head. "I was worried something like this might happen." He looked at the Coopers then picked up the copy of the news article and folded it. "Despite his desperate measures, Donovan has kept his word about this photograph. He didn't show it to me...I sort of showed it to him."

"Explain," Martía said. She took the paper from him as if it were a bargaining chip.

Fairbanks conceded. "In his quest to be appointed to practically every position there is in Sugar Pine Station—I think he has his eye on the Mayor's seat actually—Donovan was doing some research at the newspaper office a couple of years ago. I was helping him dig through the archives for information on the opening of Route 222, when we came across the story about these Gypsies."

All four glanced at each other around the table. Tommy continued, "I wasn't here then, of course, so I didn't make the connection. But Huckly, now, well he stared at that picture and finally asked me if the young couple looked familiar. Once I saw what he was on to, I had to admit, the resemblance was uncanny. He was convinced it was you, but I told him it was probably just relatives of yours, seeing as how a lot of Gypsies probably intermarry with their cousins and such." He gulped. "No offense, mind you."

Martía waved it off and unfolded the paper; they all stared at it again in silence.

"Do you have any idea what Huckly is looking

for?" Tommy gently asked the three of them.

In a soft voice, barely above a whisper, Martía replied, "Yes. I'm afraid we do."

Dolly caught the gleam of the newshound in Tommy's eye and quickly tried to change the subject. "I, uh, think I'll agree to that interview, Mr. Fairbanks. After all, I wouldn't want to pass up any free publicity. The Hut, like any business, needs customers. They don't appear like magic, you know." She grimaced at the unintentional reference.

Tommy narrowed his eyes, then sat back, reflecting. The Coopers remained tight lipped. "Well, I can certainly understand your reluctance to talk. If our roles were reversed, I'd be cautious too. But to someone like me, all this is very very interesting to say the least. I respect your silence, though. Keep your secrets for now. But you better be prepared, Donovan will be back, you can count on it."

The others looked at the editor with alarm. "Are you threatening us?" Rohan asked.

"No, no. You misunderstand. I'm on your side, though the reporter in me is screaming for a story. I just happen to have an inkling as to what he's after."

"Tell us," Ma Tutt demanded.

"Well you see, I was at the courthouse a few weeks back digging through the public records for any juicy tidbits I could use in my column, 'All About Town.'"

Dolly gave him a withering look. "I know what juicy tidbits go into that gossip column of yours.

Hmm, come to think of it, I was mentioned once or twice when I first moved to town. 'Valley Girl Buys Bakery, Wants to Add More Sugar to Sugar Pine Station.'"

"You have to admit, it's a catchy tag line," he said hopefully. Ma harrumphed.

"Anyway! I was at the courthouse and Donovan was just leaving. He rushed past me with barely a hello and a goofy grin plastered across that mug of his. I asked Lanette, the clerk, what Huckly was so excited about. She wasn't sure, but said he'd been looking at mineral rights and property lines and such. Then I remembered, from a few years ago when we were researching old newspaper articles, he showed a very keen interest in the area's old abandoned gold mines."

They stared at him in amazement.

"So if you ask me," Tommy went on, leaning forward, "it seems pretty clear what your secret is. If I'm right, do I get an exclusive interview?"

Dolly's thoughts were awhirl. Gold! Could that be what this was really all about? She looked at Rohan and Martía. They seemed sincere enough, but she didn't really know them all that well. Were they harboring more secrets? What was really in that basement of hers? Could this be some elaborate ploy to get the Hut back? She shook off her doubts. No, these were good folk; whatever their secrets, she'd help them keep a lid on their privacy. She came to a decision.

"Mr. Fairbanks——"

"Tommy."

"Tommy, I want to thank you for warning us about Mr. Huckly and his scheming ways. If we do discover gold, you'll get your exclusive interview." This brought a smile from him and a look of relief from the Coopers. "Now, if you'll excuse us, we have to finish prepping for tomorrow, then I have to head on home. Four o'clock comes mighty early each morning."

"Of course, of course," Fairbanks said as he got up, grabbed one more cookie and took a bite. "Mm mmm, thanks again for the afternoon tea. It was verra nice of you to allow me to drop in." He started to reach for the newspaper article, but Martía pulled it close. "Ah, not a problem. You folks have a great rest of the day."

Dolly showed him to the door and locked it behind him. She turned to her friends and rolled her eyes at the departing figure. "Now don't take this the wrong way, but I just have to make sure. Is there gold in that basement?"

Her friends shook their heads, tension disappearing from their faces. Rohan said, "Not that we know of. But if Donovan thinks there is then maybe that's a good thing. Maybe he's not looking for a fountain of youth after all."

"Still, I have no idea how to stop him from nosing around," Dolly muttered.

"I do," Martía said with a sly grin on her face.

In the kitchen, a thumping of falling books accompanied the Gypsy woman's pronouncement. They filed through the swinging door and stood in front of the massive wooden hutch that owned the back wall. On the cabinet counter was Mack. He'd just pushed a slew of cookbooks and recipe cards onto the floor. He jumped down, pawed through the pile separating out one index card in particular, then sat up and meowed his explanation. He started bathing, immediately unconcerned about his audience.

"What in heaven's name is this?" Dolly scolded. "If you wanted a kitty treat, you could have simply asked."

But Martía was already kneeling beside the tabby, studying the cards. She pulled the one out from under his front paws and looked at it. "Why thank you, Mack. This is exactly the one I had in mind." She petted the kitty and got up, showing it to the others. Dolly leaned in, reading the card: Forgettable Pie.

"Um, I'm not an expert on marketing, Martía, but it seems to me you'd want to advertise a pie as 'Unforgettable'—you know, as in it tastes so good, they'll always remember it."

"Ah, but this pie won't let you remember," she said with sly humor.

Dolly's eyes widened in understanding. "Now this is the kind of recipe you want to have handy in case of an emergency. And I say what we have brewing here with Donovan is definitely an emergency."

Rohan chuckled, scooched Mack out of the way and started cleaning up the mess. "You two have fun. I'll finish up here and take Mack for a walk. We're going to drop in and say hello to Father Aguilera."

The two women were already busy setting out mixing bowls and measuring cups. They readily shooed both males out of the kitchen.

"Give him our best," Dolly said absently, intent now on the list of ingredients. To her baking partner, "Looks like a standard recipe for an apple pie. But what's this one here? Looks like some kind of liquid extract. We need one drop. Are you sure that will even make a difference?"

"It will make all the difference," Martía assured her. She went to the cabinet, opened the cupboard, and searched through the selection of unlabeled jars. "Ah, here we are." Picking out a clear vial of liquid, she opened it and took a whiff, nodding in satisfaction.

Dolly caught a scent of it and said, "Slightly vanilla. Wonder if tastes like vanilla."

Martía quickly recapped the ampoule. "You don't want to taste it, let me warn you. In fact, it's best to stay away from any of these spices here. They can have disastrous effects if not used properly. That's one reason I didn't label them. I figured no one would experiment with an unknown ingredient."

"Now you tell me!" Martía flashed her a look of mild concern. Ma grimaced. "Another long story."

"We have time," the Gypsy woman said with an

encouraging smile. "And we also have the ingredients to make two pies. One will be 'Forgettable' and the other—without any special ingredients, mind you—we'll call Unforgettable, as you suggest. A product test, if you will."

"A delightfully delicious plan."

As they set about making the two apple pies, Dolly shared her slightly nightmarish experience trying to bake the Memory Cake using an unlabeled spice in place of the proper one, *Memoria*. They both laughed about the near disaster from the safe distance that time often provides.

"…And so I labeled the jar 'Nightmare' so I wouldn't be tempted to use it again," Dolly said as she finished her story.

"You were wise to throw the cake away. You would have had anxious visions for days if you'd taken just one bite. The spice you used is called *Anxiety*, and a quarter pinch is all you need. The aroma alone, during the mixing and baking process, is enough to cause one to fret."

"Ah, now that explains it. I had my panicked vision right after putting the cake in the oven." Dolly thought back to another recipe that had gone horribly wrong. "Come to think of it, the aroma of another one of your spices—which I didn't measure properly either!—caused quite a stir as well."

She then launched into another long story about the Irresistible Doughnuts and how she first met Tommy Fairbanks, who sat at her counter just crazy in love with those deep fried wonders! This brought another round of laughter from both women.

"I think he still has some love in his heart, Ma," Martía said with a wink. "And it's not all about your baking, either. Could it be the feeling is mutual?"

Dolly blushed. She had to admit, the man was handsome. But surely she didn't have any feelings for him. Did she? Was that why he appeared in her nervous vision following her ill-fated attempt at making the Memory Cake? Was her subconscious trying to tell her something? Hmm, she would have to think about that one.

As they wrapped up their two pie projects, Dolly grabbed the vial of liquid and handed it to Martía. "Here, you better do the honors. I'm afraid I might put in an extra drop."

The Gypsy woman took the stopper from the flask and squeezed one drop into the apple filling that would go into the Forgettable Pie. She steered clear of the other pie altogether. "Let's remember which one is which!"

Once the pies were in the oven, Martía went through the pantry with Dolly explaining the various spices and their 'magical' effects. She promised to help Ma organize the index cards and offered a running commentary on what had worked and what hadn't. More stories of recipes gone wild emerged and the women's laughter and encouragement worked its own kind of magic, and their friendship grew.

Soon the aroma of apple pies filled the kitchen.

Alarmed, Dolly said, "Oh no, the smell! Won't we start forgetting things? Doesn't the magic kick in during the baking process?"

"Ah, no need to worry. We added enough cinnamon to counteract that particular side effect. The aroma will not harm us. Can't you smell the cinnamon mixing with the apples?"

Dolly nodded and remembered how dusting her Irresistible Doughnuts with cinnamon had acted as a kind of neutralizing agent against the *Iseult* spice. She also remembered how dusting the mesmerized mob with cinnamon powder had broken the spell completely.

"But if someone eats a piece of pie...?"

Martía assured her. "One slice of Forgettable Pie and Donovan will no longer remember why he came to inspect the basement. But we have to serve it to him when he has that purpose in mind. The more he's obsessed with something, the more likely he'll forget it once he eats the pie."

"No need to worry about that. He's definitely obsessed with that basement and evicting me so he can discover its secret. Plus, whenever he shows up, he's always looking for a handout. Serving him a slice of pie will be...a piece of cake!"

The timer went off and Martía checked their prizes with a toothpick. "I think they're done!"

"And they're both beautiful! How do you get your crusts to come out so flaky without getting overdone?"

"A family secret. Tell me how you make such perfect bear claws and we'll call it even." The ladies shared a sisterly hug before each of them put on a pair of oven mitts and retrieved the pies from the oven.

No sooner were the steaming creations in their hands when they heard a banging on the front door. Flustered, Dolly said, "Here, let's put them in the serving window to cool." The shelf between the kitchen and the dining room prep area was just wide enough for the two pies to sit side by side.

The banging continued and Ma finally glanced at the front door. It was Donovan Huckly, face up against the glass window, glaring at them. She glared back but went ahead and opened it.

He was alone and wearing his steel gray work shirt. *Building Inspector.* He got right down to business. "I'm afraid we're going to have to shut down the Hut immediately. You have some foundation problems in that basement of yours that are of grave concern, a grave concern indeed. A safety hazard." He offered up his clipboard. "If you'll just sign here to acknowledge the results of last week's inspection."

"Now wait just one darned minute," Dolly exclaimed. "Where's your supervisor? You said last time that *he* had to inspect the basement before you came to any final decision."

Donovan shifted his feet back and forth. "Well, my supervisor…had pressing business to attend to. Yes, that's it. But he authorized me, based on my preliminary report, to act on his behalf." He tried holding Dolly's gaze, but failed. "You'll be closed for only a week or two," he added, lamely.

*Harrumph.* "We'll just see about that! Let's head over to City Hall right now and find out what he has to say." She took off her apron and balled it up, ready to stuff it in Huckly's mouth.

"Ahem, Ma? Are you forgetting something?" Martía indicated the cooling pies with a toss of her head.

"Oh! Um, yes. That's right..." Dolly grimaced, trying to calm herself and keep with the plan. "City Hall, yes. Ah, but first...Donovan...how about a piece of...uh, some good ol' fashioned apple pie? How does that sound?"

"Well, I'm not really in the mood for pie, maybe an éclair, if you have one."

Dolly shot her coconspirator a panicked look. "But this is fresh baked, right out of the oven." As if on cue, Martía brought one of the pies over along with a plate and fork. She served the unwelcomed guest a piece, the warm apple filling releasing a slight tail of steam.

"Well, if you insist." Donovan sat at a table and dug in. "Mind if I have a glass of milk?"

"Certainly," Dolly said as she went to the refrigerator, pulling Martía with her. She lowered her voice so only the Gypsy woman could hear. "Is that the right pie? I thought the forgettable potion was in the other one!"

Uncertainty played in Martía's eyes. "I thought so, but we'll know in a few moments. He should show confusion as to why he's here as soon as he finishes eating."

"I hope you're right!" Ma brought out a cold glass of milk.

Huckly polished off the rest of his pie and gulped down the milk in one long draw. "Ahh. That hit the spot." He pushed the plate toward the center of the table and sighed in satisfaction. "Now about that basement of yours."

The two women stared at the building inspector, mouths agape.

He looked over his shoulder, uncertain. "Um, thanks for the pie, by the way," he said. They continued to stare, eyes wide as well. He fidgeted. "It was really good. Honest to Pete." They stared some more. He twisted his napkin. "Best apple pie I've had in a long time." Still they waited. He gulped. "Ever." Silence. He gave it one last shot. "I'll never forget it as a long as I live. I promise."

*Ach!* "How about another piece?" Dolly motioned for Martía to bring the other pie. "We made two! You'll have to tell us which one you like best—"

"Look, now Ma, no offense. But if you think you can bribe me out of closing down this business, you can just forget it!"

Dolly's dander went up. "And if you think we're going to give in without talking to your supervisor, then *you* can just forget it!"

The two glared at each other like opposing jousters at a Renaissance Fair. Donovan blinked first. "Oh, all right. I'll talk to him again and we'll be back tomorrow. You can count on that!" He threw his napkin on the table and stormed out.

Ma threw up her hands. "It didn't work!"

"I must have served him the wrong pie," Martía cried. "I'm so sorry."

"Well, there's nothing we can do about it now. I think we should run by the parsonage and talk with Father Aguilera. He'll know what to do." Ma was almost crying in frustration.

Her friend tried to comfort her with a pat on the back. "Look, we'll try again tomorrow. We'll set the right pie aside and when he drops in again, we'll be ready." Though the words rang hollow to Dolly, she acquiesced. "Here, let's put them on the counter to finish cooling and drop in to see Father. Rohan and Mack are probably still there. Maybe they'll have some advice as well."

Dolly smiled at that. Mack would surely have something to say! "Okay, sounds like a plan." She put a toothpick in the one they'd served Donovan. "At least we'll know which one's which!" The ladies quickly straightened up out front and Ma hit the lights after locking the front door. They made sure the oven was off, then left out the back.

Within a few minutes they were outside the rectory. The door to the priest's humble abode was open as usual on a summer day. It was late afternoon, creeping into early evening and the mountain air was fresh with pine and promise.

"Hello?" Ma called.

"Hello!" came Father Aguilera's response. "We're in the kitchen as usual."

At the table sat Rohan and the priest. Even Mack was occupying a chair, though he was fast asleep and not participating in the conversation at the moment. Martía and Dolly pulled up two more chairs and sat down.

"Oh boy, do we have a story to tell you," Ma said. And within fifteen minutes the two men were caught up on the saga.

"My, oh my," the priest said. "I guess my little attempt at blackmail didn't work then, because he assured me yesterday after church that he wasn't going to try and shut you down."

"What do you mean?"

"I don't have any deep or dark secret to hang over him, but whenever he starts to make a nuisance of himself around town, I gently reminded him of his long term dream of becoming mayor of Sugar Pine Station. He knows that if he ruffles too many feathers, it'll be harder for him to win the election in a few years."

"Evidently, he prizes whatever he thinks is in my basement more than anything else."

"Yes, he's consumed by greed," Rohan said. "In the clutches of a Deadly Sin."

They all nodded in sad agreement.

The priest offered, "If only he could let go of this obsession. He's not a bad sort, actually...."

Before anyone else could add another commentary, Big Ben's voice rang out. "Halloooo! Anyone home?" The mountain man's head appeared at the open kitchen window. "Is that you, Ma?" A look of relief in his eyes. He nodded at the Coopers in greeting.

The priest said, "Come on in, we can make room."

"Actually, I came to get Ma. Someone's broken into the Hut. Back door's been busted wide open and I thought I saw someone snooping around up front in the dining area."

"What? Oh no!" Dolly was the first out of her chair and led the crew as they all scrambled back to the Hut. Even Mack padded after them after being rudely awakened from his late afternoon nap.

As they approached the front door, Big Ben said, "Best be careful, Ma." But she was already peering in through the tinted glass door. After a long moment, she stepped back and scratched her head. Each of them went up to the plate glass window and stared. They too shook their heads in confusion after witnessing the scene.

Ma unlocked the front door, though Benjamin Reed insisted on entering first just in case the man inside did anything unexpected. He needn't have worried. Donovan Huckly was wandering around the dining room in a daze. He sat down at one table then got up and moved to another. After a moment he heaved himself up and headed over to the glass display case, staring at the empty shelves. He stared at the ceiling. He rubbed his chin. Eventually he took note of the audience gaping at him in disbelief.

"Where am I?" he said. "Who am I? Who are you?" His face was messy with pie crumbs and mushy bits of fruit. His shirt was stained with globs of apple filling.

"Oh my lands!" Dolly saw the pies on the counter. Both were half eaten! Her face fell; the toothpick was missing and the desserts were out of place. She wasn't sure which one was the Forgettable Pie. "Donovan! You ate practically a whole pie. What were you thinking?"

A ripple of clarity worked its way up from the recesses of his mind. "I had to see which one tasted the best," he said in a vacant voice. "Like when I judged at the County Fair…." He smiled at the distant memory, eyes gazing at something only he could see. He turned back to Dolly. "They both deserve a blue ribbon, Ma!" He blinked then frowned, cognition slipping away once more.

Dolly quickly explained to Father Aguilera that one of the pies contained that 'special ingredient.' *Wink wink.* She didn't want to say more since Big Ben was in the room, but the priest understood. "But now we don't know which one's which!" she whispered.

A jingle at the front door announced a new

arrival. Tommy Fairbanks, hot on the trail of a story, entered, his keen eyes taking in the scene. "Howdy, folks. Just heard you had a break in. Everyone all right? Any suspects yet? Anything stolen...from the basement?" he added knowingly, sniffing for anything juicy.

The sudden appearance of the newsman and his flurry of questions had everyone momentarily at a loss for words. What was their story? How were they going to spin this? Did Donovan find anything before eating the pies? Was the Cooper's secret going to be exposed at last?

Martía was the first to recover and she took charge with a few simple commands. "Why don't we all just sit down and relax for a moment. Rohan, please check the back room, make sure everything is okay. Ben, could you push some tables together? Ma, would you mind making some coffee? Donovan, here's a napkin. Maybe you can wipe your face?"

Tommy raised an eyebrow at the Inspector General's messy appearance. He then noticed the pies on the counter and inhaled deeply. "Yes, let's everyone sit down and relax. Wonderful idea. You can fill me in on the details of the break in over some coffee and pie. Mind if I help myself to a piece?"

Before Ma could stop him, the editor picked up a fork and slid a slice of apple pie onto a plate. He took a spot at one of the tables Ben had arranged and dug in. Everyone else held their breaths.

"Ah, yes," Tommy said with his mouth full, "it's

verra good."

The rest of the gang slowly made their way round the hungry newspaper editor. Like a participant at a pie eating contest, Tommy couldn't stop until the last bite disappeared. The man loved his food. He finally set down his fork, wiped his mouth, and looked up at the small crowd that had gathered to watch him eat.

"Can I help you?" He glanced around, eyes uncertain. "Where are we, by the way? Surely not my office. Oh, are we having a party?"

Martía said, "Yes. Yes we are. Ma, bring the other pie. We can celebrate at last!"

Everyone pulled up a chair while Dolly brought out plates, forks, and some mugs along with a pot of fresh coffee. Rohan returned from the back with two more guests, running friends Jo and Kelli. They were dressed for an evening jog.

"Hey, we were out and about and saw your back door propped open," Kelli said. "And we heard the word party," Jo added. "Mind if we join the fun?"

"Not at all," Dolly said as she cut the remaining half of the normal pie into four pieces and served them to Father Aguilera, Big Ben, Kelli, and Jo. Tommy and Rohan waved off the offer and Donovan was too dazed to notice he'd been bypassed. In fact, he was looking a little queasy sitting next to the priest.

"Aren't you two having any?" Ben asked. "There's almost a half a pie left." He indicated the second pie pan on the counter.

"Oh, we sort of nibbled along the way as we baked them," Ma said noncommittally. This was true; she did share a slice of apple with Martía when they first began their project a few hours earlier. "Plus, we don't want to spoil our appetite. It's almost dinner time."

The runners looked at their watches and got up as did Fairbanks, who said, "I guess I should be going too. I have a column to write before we go to press this week. Ma, I still want an interview about your success with the Hut." He scratched his chin. "Seems like there was something else I was going to ask you. Huh. Well, probably wasn't important anyway."

"No, probably wasn't," Dolly murmured. Martía stifled a giggle.

"Can we help clean up?" Kelli asked.

"We're fine, really" Ma replied. "But can one of you make sure Donovan gets home all right? He's looking a little peaked."

"I can do that," Big Ben said. "I pass right by his place on my way home."

"What brought you back into town, by the way?" asked Father Aguilera. "You were just here on Saturday." Ben Reed usually trekked down from his log cabin hideaway only every few weeks or so. "Forgot to buy some toothpaste. I'm a mountain man, but I like to keep my breath fresh…for the ladies." He winked at Kelli and Jo, who blushed.

"Seems we're all prone to a bit of forgetfulness every now and then," Dolly said, offering an insider elbow poke at her co-baker.

Goodbyes were soon exchanged along with plenty of *thank yous* and a *let's do it again sometime*. Finally, all those who had dropped in unexpectedly shuffled out the door leaving Dolly, Rohan, Martía, and Father Aguilera sitting at the table, exhausted. Mack was nowhere to be seen.

The priest said, "I'm not at all hungry for dinner and I'm actually getting sleepy. You sure there were no special ingredients in the pie we finished off, Ma?"

"Just the ingredients of good friends and fellowship, I think." She smiled at her three confidants. "Those form a magical mix that will relax you every time. Too bad we have more work to do tonight. Rohan, can you fix the back door again, please?"

"Certainly."

Martía squeezed her husband's hand. "Oh, and did you look in the basement? Did that nosey inspector discover anything?"

"Nothing was disturbed as far as I could tell. The cellar walls are solid; the hidden spring is still plugged up after all these years. I think Mr. Huckly must have eaten the Forgettable Pie before starting his search."

"I wonder what he was actually looking for," Dolly said, pondering the mystery. "Mr. Fairbanks thought it was gold. But Donovan sure was suspicious of your youthful appearance."

"We may never know," Father Aguilera said, "now that our friend has lost all interest in that basement of yours. By the way, what *was* the secret ingredient that caused Tommy and Donovan to forget their obsessions? You must have used a jar of the stuff, whatever it was."

"No, just a single drop of *Lethe*," Martía said as if no other explanation was needed.

The priest thought for a moment and nodded. "Ah, yes. *'Far off from these, a slow and silent stream, Lethe, the river of oblivion, rolls her watery labyrinth.'*"

Dolly looked at her saintly guest with furrowed brows. "Okay, I know it's a quote, but you'll have to enlighten me, Father. I'm clueless as to the reference."

"John Milton, in Paradise Lost. He was referring to one of the five rivers in Hades, Lethe, the River of Forgetfulness."

"Ah, well sure, forgetfulness. I never knew. I guess I've only heard of the River Styx."

"That would be the River of Hate," Rohan said. "And a dangerous elixir best left out of all recipes."

"No argument there," Dolly said. "Sounds dangerous indeed. I hope *Styx* isn't in one of the unlabeled bottles you left in the pantry." Martía shook her head, much to Ma's relief. "But how did Milton describe the River Lethe, Father? A river of oblivion?"

The priest explained, "The Latin word for forgetfulness is oblivion, a kind of stupor where one has no memory of joy or sorrow."

Dolly nodded. "Well, that certainly describes Mr.

Huckly's state right now. He's definitely oblivious to the events of these past few months. I'm a bit worried for him, though. He can't even remember who he is, including his various civic duties. I was kind of getting used to his different colored shirts. Are you sure he'll be all right?"

"Oh, he'll sleep off most of his confusion by tomorrow," Martía said. "But what has obsessed him the most will be gone from his memory for good."

"If he needs help remembering his name, you can always make him a certain spice cake, you know. He'll eat anything if it's free or on sale," Father Aguilera said, while everyone tried not to laugh at Donovan's expense.

As they began clearing the dishes, Ma said, "I'm just happy everything turned out all right in the end. I think I've had my fill of special spices and secret ingredients for quite some time. I could use a break from all the excitement!"

Just then a knock and a rattle rang out from the kitchen followed by a series of bangs and bumps as jars and bottles hit the floor. Fortunately no clatter of broken glass accompanied the noisy racket. But soon a string of demanding meows, chirrups, and yowls made their way into the dining room as Mack announced his entrance, pushing and batting a small tin of something or other through the swinging door.

"Oh no, not again!" Dolly exclaimed. She got up and hurried over to where the tabby was wrestling with his prize, intent on opening the lid. She pried the tin from the ornery cat's paws and read the label. "Catnip! *Whew!* Now that's a relief!"

Mack *mreowwed* impatiently and pawed up the side of Dolly's leg, arguing for the immediate release of his special mix of herbs. This led to a quiet laugh. Rohan motioned that he'd be right back; then returned momentarily with a mouse-shaped toy. The yowls grew louder as Ma opened the can and stuffed a pinch of catnip into the kitty plaything.

"Here you go, mister." She handed Mack the toy mouse and his impatient scoldings immediately gave way to a surge of contented purrs.

"Simple pleasures," Rohan said, smiling.

The priest shook his head in wonder. "Why cats gush over that particular aroma, I'll never know. But it certainly has the power to calm the wild beast."

"Must be magic," teased Martía.

Everyone chuckled, enjoying the moment. Ma considered her friends and whispered a prayer of thanksgiving for all the blessings in her life. She wiped her eyes, tears of love and gratitude quick to fall, as she looked fondly upon her feline companion.

"Just lay off the real magic for a little bit," Dolly said, trying to sound stern. "That's all I ask."

But Mack was too busy nuzzling his catnip toy to pay any attention to such silly human requests.

## The End

## *Ma's Favorite Recipes*

~*~

## Ma's Irresistible 'Puff Ball' Doughnuts

Ingredients: 3 eggs, 1 cup of sugar, 3 cups of milk, ½ teaspoon of salt, ½ teaspoon of nutmeg, 2 teaspoons of baking powder, about 4 cups of flour. All-vegetable shortening for frying. Cinnamon sugar.

Preparation: Gently beat sugar into eggs, slowly adding milk; combine flour, baking powder, nutmeg, and salt; add dry ingredients into the liquid, mixing until doughy (add more flour if needed). Heat 2 to 3 inches of all-vegetable shortening (like Crisco) in a deep saucepan to 365 degrees F.

Step 1: Drop by spoonfuls into heated shortening, careful not to splatter. Turn doughnut holes with wooden spoon until evenly browned. Remove to paper towels and place on rack to cool.

Step 2: Sprinkle with cinnamon sugar to taste. Another idea is to serve with vanilla bean ice cream. Eat when warm. They're irresistible!*

## Ma's Memorable Spice Cake

Ingredients: 2 ½ cups of flour, ¼ cup of cornstarch, 4 teaspoons of baking powder, ½ teaspoon of salt, ½ teaspoon of nutmeg, ½ teaspoon of allspice, ½ teaspoon of cloves, 1 teaspoon of ginger, 1 teaspoon of cinnamon (all spices ground), 2 cups brown sugar, 3 eggs, 1 cup of milk, 2 teaspoons of vanilla, 1 cup of unsalted butter (softened).

Preparation: Preheat oven to 350 degrees F. Spray then lightly flour a 9 x 13 inch cake pan. Combine dry ingredients, including spices but not the brown sugar, in a large mixing bowl. Mix eggs, milk, and vanilla in a separate bowl. Set aside brown sugar.

Step 1: Gently beat softened butter into dry ingredients until mixture forms pebble-like granules. Slowly add about half of the liquid mixture and beat on low until smooth. Add brown sugar and mix in the other half of the liquid; beat on medium for about 30 seconds.

Step 2: Pour batter into cake pan. Bake for about 35 to 40 minutes. Test with toothpick by sticking into cake center; it should come out clean. Remove cake pan, let cool for about 5 minutes. Serve warm with vanilla bean ice cream. Great conversation and wonderful memories are sure to follow!*

## Ma's Unforgettable Apple Pie

Ingredients: 5 to 6 medium apples (Granny Smiths are great, Fujis are fine), ¾ cup of sugar, 2 tablespoons of flour, 1½ teaspoons of ground cinnamon, 1 tablespoon of regular butter. Purchase your favorite ready-made double crust pie dough. For the top of the pie crust, you'll also need 1 egg white (lightly beaten) and cinnamon sugar.

Prep the Pie Filling: Peel, core, and slice the apples into small to medium wedges. Mix dry ingredients together: sugar, flour, and cinnamon. Toss the apple slices in the dry ingredients, coat slices completely.

Prep the Pie Plate: Spray then lightly flour a 9 inch pie plate, roll out the disc for the bottom crust, press to fit the pie plate then trim excess. Set aside the top crust.

Step 1: Preheat oven to 400 degrees F. Pour the apple slices into the unbaked pie crust, sprinkling the rest of the dry ingredients throughout. Dot apple filling with butter.

Step 2: Cover the apple filling with the top crust; seal and flute the edges. Brush the crust with egg white, then slit the crust so steam can escape when baking. Sprinkle top crust with cinnamon sugar. Bake

30 to 40 minutes until golden brown and apples are tender. Serve warm with vanilla bean ice cream and enjoy with friends and family. It'll be an unforgettable experience!*

~*~

* As you know, there are no such spices as *Iseult* or *Memoria,* nor are there liquid drops of *Lethe.* These are fictional ingredients mentioned only in the novel. Feel free to experiment with the recipes above, however, tailoring them to your particular taste. But please don't republish them exactly as they appear here.

## *Two Q&As With Lyn Perry*

Fellow writer Jeff Chapman sat down with me, so to speak, and threw me some softball questions. For which I'm grateful.

### 1) How does it feel to complete and publish your first novel?

Relieved! I'm a starter of projects and have a hard time completing them. So to see a story through and not leave it at a cliff-hanger of an ending (which I'm oft times wont to do!) is satisfying. It tells me I can do it again – and this time with a longer work.

It's funny, I started out writing micro-fiction a few years ago, then flash fiction. I graduated to short stories and then novellas. But with this short novel (which is actually four short novellas tied together forming a complete story arc) I think I've learned how to structure a complete, full-length novel. I'm excited to get started on the next book. Oops, that spoils my answer to your last question, so I'll talk more about that later.

### 2) Why a donut hut?

Last summer I took an online writing workshop hosted by Dean Wesley Smith. The topic was "Ideas to Story." The big take-away for me was that ideas for stories are everywhere. All you need is a character in a setting with a problem.

It sounds simple, but practically all stories reveal within the first chapter (or even within the first 500 words) some tension that needs resolution by the main character. An idea, then, is not a full blown plot and it's not how everything comes together in the end. An idea is simply "what happens next" once you have the character in a setting with a problem.

One of the writing assignments, then, for this workshop was to just look around at the ordinary places and things in your life and connect them into a 500 word opening. We had a few other ingredients to include, but basically this forms the beginning idea for a story.

So I took my notebook, headed for the local Krispy Kreme for a little sugar-induced inspiration, and as I was eating my doughnut, I looked around and thought why not? It's a setting. And then there was a retirement age woman who was behind the counter, and I wondered if she *wanted* to be working or *had* to be. Well, that was the character in a setting with a problem (forced to work at 65, yikes!).

Now according to Kate Wilhelm (or so I learned via Dean Smith), you dismiss the first two iterations on that idea and go with the third. My third take on this idea was a semi-retired mother figure in a donut shop in a small mountain community with a magical cat that got her into trouble as much as he helped her out. Voila. Ma Tutt's Donut Hut. Not sure that's the best idea I could have come up with, but I liked it so I ran with it.

**3) Have you tried any of Ma Tutt's recipes? Without the magical, unmarked spices, I assume.**

Correct, the mystery spices I used in the book don't exist. Which is good news! I wouldn't want to be responsible for the potentially drastic effects of *Iseult* or *Lethe* (read the book to find out what they can do…or google them!).

But I have to admit, I've not tried the specific recipes I've included in the appendix. Now my mother-in-law sent me her family spice cake recipe, so I assume it's good to go. And I found the puff ball donut recipe in an old Pennsylvania Dutch cookbook – old enough that there probably aren't any copyright issues. But I tweaked it and the generic apple pie recipe just in case!

Now my wife and I have made spice cake and apple pie before, however. We like to bake and do well in the kitchen together. So the culinary setting isn't out of our realm of experience. Neither is the feline connection as we have two cats. Though we make no claims about being magical, I did follow the rule 'write what you know' – at least to a certain extent!

**4) Cozy mysteries featuring cats are a dime a baker's dozen. What separates your book from the crowd?**

That's a good one. Heck, what separates any of these series from each other? I was in B&N the other day and counted no less than 10 Cat Cozy Mystery

Series. There were cats in a bookstore, in a bakery, in a library, detective cats, magical cats... I was both discouraged and encouraged at the same time.

First, a bit discouraged because I realized that I was in a crowded category so knew I wasn't cornering the market. Shoot, I probably hadn't even come up with a unique subgenre – a magical cat in a coffee shop! (Maybe I should add a bookstore to the café!)

But then I thought, hey, this is a wildly popular genre. People love gentle mysteries featuring loveable cats and a quirky cast of characters in a small town setting that reminds them of the place they'd love to retire to. And yet... most of these stories feature a dead body in every episode. I mean, really, Angela Lansbury must have cleaned out the whole village of Cabot Cove!

So I got to thinking, is there room for a *gentle* gentle cozy? One that features a bit of mystery and suspense, but no dead bodies? One where the characters and their interactions move the story forward as much as Mack the Magical Cat and the mystery spice ingredient he introduces in each episode does? I think so. I'm not saying there will never be a dead body, but I'm sort of tired of that cliché and think there are other mysteries out there to solve. Plus, I readily admit to weaving into my stories gentle spiritual themes of love and friendship and forgiveness and the power of life over death. This may be what distinguishes my stories the most from what's out there currently.

**5) Ma Tutt's local business is in direct competition with the Creamy Pie, a national franchise across the road. What's going on with the David versus Goliath theme?**

Here's a paragraph from my novel that explains Ma's attitude (and mine, to a certain degree, though I know one can't stop 'progress').

*Creamy Pie! Dolly fumed. The homogenization of America was what it was. Small towns losing their quaint little charm; architecturally unique, if sometimes odd and curious, buildings giving way to big box stores and generic storefronts. Pretty soon, every city across the country would blur into one bland mess of retail malls, boring restaurants, and office buildings.*

Now I have nothing against Walmart or McDonalds, per se. Companies like these have their place in our society and provide millions of jobs and infuse billions of dollars into our economy. But they aren't the be-all and end-all of America either. And thus the reason for the small town, one-of-a-kind restaurant, retail store, or service business.

A place like Ma Tutt's is part of the fabric of our country. People who run places like this work incredibly long and hard hours and since I don't want to do the actual work of owning a doughnut shop, I'll simply live vicariously through Ma who will do all the grunt work for me.

**6) One of the strengths of your novel is the endearing characters who gather at Ma's Donut**

**Hut. My favorites are Father Emilio Aguilera and the wacky villain Donovan Huckly. Which characters did you enjoy the most?**

I like Donovan as well. He's not a bad sort. He's nosy, a know-it-all, and has aspirations. So he'll continue to play the role of annoying interrupter. Has that bit of a "huckster" vibe going on as well, thus his last name. I think of him as a kind of young Mr. Haney from Green Acres who always has an angle.

Of course, I love Ma Tutt, who has many of the loving attributes (and fantastic baking skills!) of my mother-in-law. And yes, Father Aguilera is a kind and endearing spiritual leader, the type of person I'd like to be.

But another character, which may be my favorite (besides Mack who happens to look a lot like our indoor kitty Izzy), is Martía Cooper, the Gypsy wife of Rohan. We get to know them both a little bit in this novel, but I'm so enamored with their background and way of life, that she and her husband will get their own tale in the next novel.

Speaking of which…

**7) I think Mack has a few more lives. Are there more Ma Tutt/Mack stories in the oven?**

Yes. I've started work on the next novel already. The magical spices that Martía left at the Hut and the intuitive nature of Mack simply begs for more tales. And if you haven't surmised by now, this premise serves as the conceit for most of my stories in this series. Some kind of ingredient mix up results in some kind of trial and is resolved by some kind of feline intervention. Not sophisticated, I admit, but I think engaging and winsome. The reader will have to let me know!

Plus, I think for this next book at least, I'll stick with a similar structure as the first book. I like the episodic nature of these stories – they're stand alones but tied together with an overarching plotline. One can read a chapter as a complete story at bedtime and be satisfied, but also want to keep reading to see where the larger story goes next. At least, that's my hope. Thanks for reading!

## Another Q&A

When another fellow writer, Lisa Godfrees, asked if she could host an interview, who was I to refuse? Here are her questions and my replies.

**1) The first question I ask everyone is this: Do you consider yourself a Christian author or author of Christian fiction? What do you think the difference is?**

I'll clarify the first option so we're on the same page – I'm a Christian who happens to like to write. I think the term author is somewhat static and so try to avoid it. I like the term writer. That is, 'author' seems to focus on who the person is instead of what they do. (Not a difference worth quibbling about, but one that has been helpful for me in my writing journey).

That being said, I am a Christian (my identity is in Christ) and what I do at this point in my life is teach middle school, write when I can, and drink coffee. As for what I write, it runs the gamut. I dabble in a wide variety of genres – including humor, speculative fiction, supernatural suspense, thriller, and now lately, with my first short novel under my belt, cozy mystery.

Although I might classify some of my fiction as "Christian" (often redemptive in nature, and touching on things of eternity) I presume most would consider it spiritually thematic, a looser term granted. It's not that I dislike the phrase Christian fiction, but how that term is used in Christian publishing circles probably doesn't describe what I currently write.

The difference, in my mind, is that 'Christians who write' is the bigger category. One genre in which Christians who write might find themselves is Christian fiction (where Christ is central to the lives of the main characters and the Gospel message is fairly evident). I've not yet published a story with this particular emphasis, but I'm open to it.

In fact, I'm collaborating right now with a fairly popular Christian author who writes Christian fiction and we'll be releasing a cozy mystery in a few months. It's set in Western Kansas and ties into some of her other previously published novels. I'm very excited, but will have to keep mum for now. Maybe we can do another interview when that one gets published!

**2) Now, tell me about the cover of Ma Tutt's, because it is so very cute and appealing. How did it come about? How much input did you have into the design?**

Thanks! I thought the cover really worked as well – it matches the cozy genre quite nicely and has a cat on the front! Who can resist a cat and a bakery? As an indie writer, I'm responsible for pretty much all aspects of the publishing process. Many self-published writers farm out their covers, and that's a good option if it's affordable for one's situation.

Now I'm still on the 'conservative' (cheap) side, shall we say, so I find interesting artwork and photographs on iStockphoto.com and then will often, as was the case for Ma Tutt's cover, send an image to my son-in-law along with some ideas for layout and then he'll design the rest. He crafted a silhouette of a cat, placed all the elements, and found the right typography. I approved the cover and paid him real money (plus invited my daughter and him over for dinner!).

I plan for this to be a series (Mack the Magical Cat Mysteries), so I've already found other storefront bakery shots like the one I used for *Ma Tutt's Donut Hut*. The other covers will be branded similarly but with different color themes and cat silhouettes. They should be very recognizable as part of the same cozy mystery series. It's a lot of fun to see a cover come together so nicely.

**3) One of the most memorable characters in *Ma Tutt's Donut Hut* is Donovan Huckley. I had a hard time telling if he was evil or just really annoying. How would you describe Donovan's character? And what would he say to the question?**

Donovan is a great character, one of my favorites. He was going to be an out and out villain, but he just never grew into that role and I ended up thinking that he's really not a bad sort after all. Yep, he's just annoying. He's a nosy know-it-all with aspirations to become Mayor.

So he'll continue to play the role of a quirky pain in the behind. He also has that bit of a cheapskate "huckster" feel to him as well, thus his last name. If asked how he feels about being thusly described, I think he'd be offended and then ask for a free doughnut.

**4) Can you tell us something about *Ma Tutt's Donut Hut* that you know but isn't in the book? Maybe something about the Mayor, who we hear about often from Donovan but never get to meet?**

I'm still deciding whether we'll ever meet the Mayor or if he'll be that "man behind the curtain" that everyone talks about but never really knows personally. I picture him in his 70s, however, and wanting to retire after his term is up next year (setting the stage for Donovan to run), but other than that, I don't know much more about him, really.

As for some other Sugar Pine Station tidbits (fictional mountain town Sugar Pine Station is the setting, north of real life Oakhurst, CA on the way to Yosemite), I think I can only say this. There is, like Donovan suspected, an abandoned gold mine near Ma Tutt's Donut Hut. That basement has yet to reveal all of its mysteries.

## 5) What are you working on now?

Would it surprise you to learn I'm working on *Ma Tutt's Secret Spice* – Book #2 in my Mack the Magical Cat Mystery series? I plan to structure it the same way as Book #1 and include five tales of baking madness, magical ingredients, and feline intuition tied together with an overarching story line that serves as the novel's gentle mystery.

I say gentle because there are no dead bodies in either of these books and the "secret" isn't very sophisticated. But I think the characters are winsome and their interactions are fun and lively; add in a bit of suspense and I think the whole things works really well. My goal is that the ending will leave the reader entertained and satisfied. You'll have to tell me if I succeed!

## *A Word from Lyn Perry*

Thanks for reading this curious cozy. This short novel came about after writing the first tale last summer as a stand-alone short story. Now, a bakery stocked with magical spices and a mysterious cat obviously begs for more adventures to be told.

So as I wrote my next story (which turned out to be 'Tail' Number 3), I saw a larger story arc develop. I liked the idea of an episodic novel, so I wrote two more stories, then tied all the tales together while attempting to maintain an overarching plot.

And here we are. You'll have to tell me if it worked for you or not.

As an indie published author and storyteller, I rely on word of mouth for future sales. If you liked *Ma Tutt* then I'd appreciate it if you mentioned it to a friend and/or took a moment to write a short review online. Even a few comments on Amazon or Goodreads and such would be great!

Again, thank you for your interest and support. And, of course, I'd enjoy hearing from you directly. Email me at lyngperry@yahoo.com or visit my website at www.lyndonperrywriter.com to say hi.

Also, if you are interested in reading more of my stories, the following pages list a few of my books. Most are available as ebooks at Amazon, others via your favorite bookseller. Enjoy!

## *More Speculative Fiction from Lyn Perry*

*Accidents, a Tremble Town Episode*, co-written with
Stoney M. Setzer

Newlyweds Hazel and Elwood Dell drove their
new '57 Chevy into the small community of Ichabod,
North Carolina. They should have just turned around
and left. They had no idea what dark secrets they'd
soon stumble upon - bargains with the devil that
would trap them in a place even the residents called
Tremble Town. For the Dells, their new home simply
became a lifelong nightmare...of ACCIDENTS.

*Escape!, a Max McCannor Adventure*, co-written
with T. M. Hunter

Max McCannor and his friends all suffer under
the cruelty of their orphanage headmaster. Reaching a
breaking point and spurred on by the hope of finding
his long-lost father, Max convinces the others to flee
their captors and head west. But the headmaster has
much to lose, and hires one of his former orphans to
track the children down and return them to the
orphanage before they ESCAPE for good.

*The Last Prayer – A Silo Story*

A SF Novella inspired by Hugh Howey's world
of *Wool*. In the post-apocalypse, society continues in
underground silos, kept safe from the toxic world
above by a simple hatch door and a strict set of rules.

For generations, an oligarchy of priests and politicians preserved their standing while the common workers lived in ignorance. When a young girl starts speaking of heaven as if it were just outside, the rigid caste system begins to crack. Sides are quickly drawn. The only thing preventing a violent upheaval is an old priest's confession and the child's last prayer. But will such simple faith be enough to save them all?

*The Sword of Otrim*, an epic fantasy

Otrim of Idessa is a noble barbarian, knight, and sage. Called by Queen Philipa and commissioned as lieutenant of the Leonine regiment, he and his band of warriors are off to fight the Korreti infidels. But when conflict over battlefield strategies erupts between the lieutenant and his general, the brutal Ardus Atellus, Otrim and his closest friends are accused of treason. Not only must he fight to regain his honor before the Queen, he must fight for his very life if he hopes to save the lives of his men.

*Ulemet and the Jaguar God*, a Mesoamerican fantasy

Deformed and misshapen at birth, Ulemet is ugly in a way that attracts second looks, but seldom pity. Cursed by her Olmec village elders and taunted by her people, she flees into the rainforest never to return. Rejected and alone, the young girl's only solace is her small jade carving of Uaxaca, the jaguar animal spirit she wagers will guard her as she makes her way to Tenochtitlán, the golden city of hope.

Escaping danger after danger only to be captured by slavers, Ulemet is forced to play in the ulama, the sacrificial ball game that could result in her freedom or end in her death. Will her hopes in Uaxaca prove misplaced, or will the jaguar god, who's visited her dreams as a mysterious shaman, finally prove true?

Collections...

*Last Gasp - Four Cozy Thrillers*, a collection of light horror shorts with a dash of humor.
+ Audition With a Vampire - A movie director can't believe his latest auditions.
+ Show, Don't Tell - A writer struggles with a new genre...and her muse.
+ Captain Tyler's Ghost - A local legend takes on new meaning for a hotel owner.
+ Princess and the Zombie - A father/daughter hunting trip goes terribly...right!

*Last Laugh - Four Flights of Fancy*, a collection of speculative shorts with a dash of humor.
+ Og's Greatest Invention - A Neanderthal's revolutionary concept.
+ Monkey Business - 3 Space Monkey Pirate Tales.
+ I Just About Died! - An Elf, an Ogre, and a Hollywood Party.
+ Billy Farnsworth, Zombie Hunter - Where Z-Hunting is Fun!
+ Bonus: Four Funny Tasting Treats - Microfiction

As editor…

*Dead or Alive: An Aston West Collection*
by T. M. Hunter, edited by Lyndon Perry

Ride along with Aston West, your favorite space pirate, as he treks across the galaxy in this special collection of 11 new and classic space opera tales by T. M. Hunter. This swarmy Spaceman is an Every-man, really, and embodies the best of us as well as the worst. You cheer for him, you boo him, and on rare occasions you'd like to sit down and toss back some Vladirian liquor with him. For the most part, Aston would rather just live his life, being the loner and uncaring slob he is normally. But when the chips are down, there's no one you'd rather have watching your back. In these action-packed stories you'll discover for yourself why Aston West is so often wanted either dead or alive.

*Zero Hour: Stories of Spiritual Suspense*
by Stoney M. Setzer, edited by Lyndon Perry

Are you into tales of suspense reminiscent of the days of pulp fiction? Then you'll likely enjoy this collection of stories that combine mystery, thriller, and moral themes into a family friendly volume. Think Mystery Theater with a spiritual twist! In *Zero Hour* Christian author Stoney M. Setzer pulls together an anthology of 15 Twilight Zone-like supernatural thrillers that will transport you to that shadowland where anything is possible.

## A Sneak Peek

First Love 'Tail' – "Yesterday"
from *Ma Tutt's Secret Spice*

The mountain air had a slight chill to it when Dolly and Martía met at the back door of the bakery at just after four in the morning. It was the 4th of July. Ma Tutt's Donut Hut opened at five o'clock sharp, and she had her prep time down to forty-five minutes.

"Good morning, Ma," Martía said, yawning. She gave her matronly friend a hug. "I'm glad we decided to do most of our kitchen work before leaving for the day. Those three-thirty baking sessions were starting to wear mighty thin."

Dolores Tutt chuckled. "Don't you know, the older we get, the less sleep we need! At your age, you should be able to function on just a two or three hour nap." Ma winked at her 'younger' friend, sharing an inside joke.

Martía Cooper was one hundred years old but didn't look a day past twenty-four. That's the age she and her husband Rohan stopped growing old, for some mysterious reason. The Coopers were Gypsies and Dolly, though privy to their secret, still mostly chalked the strange and wondrous happenings that surrounded them to their intriguing Romany background.

Including the presence of Mack, a very intriguing feline in his own right.

The gray Mackerel had come with the Hut when Dolly purchased the building six months before. Due to the pronounced M on the tabby's forehead, Dolly christened him Mack. He was called Tozier, however, in a previous life when he belonged to the Coopers—as much as a cat *can* belong to anyone. And he, too, was quite advanced in years, having just celebrated his sixtieth birthday. But these tales have already been told.

Dolly, for the most part, simply accepted the mystery of it all.

Mack greeted the two women with a surly *mrrow* as they entered the kitchen and hit the lights.

"Evidently, *he* doesn't like the later start time," Martía said. She found his plastic bin of food, the cat griping all the while. "It's too early for breakfast, Mack!" But she acquiesced to his demands and filled his bowl with kibble. The throaty complaints turned to a satisfied purr as he dug in.

"No such thing as too early for breakfast," Dolly said, shaking her head. "After all the time you've spent with him, you should know that by now."

"Ah, but we didn't spoil him as you have done. Cat food purchased from a store? *Oosh*, this is why he has claws. There is a mountainside to explore behind the Hut and plenty of mice for him to find."

Ma shivered at the thought. "As long as he never shows me his prize, I'll just pretend he doesn't hunt." She looked at the cute little kitty door next to the back entrance and considered herself fortunate that Mack hadn't brought back any of his kills into the kitchen. Oh, the local food and health inspector would have a fit if he were to visit on the day Mack left such an offering!

She peeled her eyes off her feline friend and grabbed a favorite apron, one with a colorful splay of California poppies. She donned a hairnet and tucked away a few graying strands of hair. Ready at last, she began her opening routine with a spry step that belied her sixty-year old legs.

"I have a feeling it's going to be a busy morning, Martía. If you'll man the oven and deep fat fryer, I'll make sure the display case out front is fully stocked." The Gypsy woman nodded and, with another yawn, got to work.

This being a Friday and the start to a busy holiday weekend in the middle of tourist season, Dolly expected quite a crowd. But then, so far this summer, most weekends boasted a whirlwind of activity. After just two months of business, the Hut was already the community's hotspot and a favorite stop for vacationers on their way to a mountain lake getaway. It was not unusual to see a line forming at the front door by the time Dolly hit the lights and turned the Closed sign to Open.

After witnessing a stifled yawn, Dolly patted the younger woman's shoulder on her way to the front of the store. "I'll bring you some coffee when it's ready."

"That would be wonderful. Thanks, Ma."

"Thank you for helping!" she called back over her shoulder. "I'm so glad you and Rohan decided to stay the summer." Dolly had only known Martía for a short time but it seemed as if they'd always been friends. They'd shared enough experiences in recent weeks to last some people a lifetime, that was for certain.

Martía *tsk tsk'd* and said in her vaguely foreign accent, "It is nothing."

To Dolores Tutt, though, this new friendship was a wonderful gift.

She'd recently moved—not knowing a soul—to Sugar Pine Station, a small mountain community nestled in the upper foothills of the Sierra Nevadas, in order to fulfill a life-long dream of owning her own baked goods and coffee shop. It was an early retirement gift to herself, but one that kept her busy from before sunrise to just past noon each day, plus a few more hours of prep only to start it all over again the next morning. Without Martía's help, she doubted she could keep up the pace come autumn.

"What are your plans for this fall, Martía?" Dolly asked as she returned to the kitchen after turning on the two forty-cup coffee machines, one decaf, one regular. Those would take an hour to percolate, so she also put on a quick four-cup pot to help jumpstart the day. "Will you and Rohan continue to travel on your own, or will you join up with another band of Gypsies?"

Martía sighed. "Given our...*youthful* condition, I suppose we'll travel on alone. Probably north to Canada. We heard about a troupe of Romany in Vancouver who are not kin, or at least distant enough to not know of us. There are still those of our immediate clan who might remember us from twenty, forty, or sixty years ago. That's one reason we must leave Sugar Pine Station soon. We lived here for almost twenty years and I'm afraid there will be people in town who will notice that we haven't aged."

This was probably true, though the only other person besides Dolly who knew of their secret was Father Emilio Aguilera, the elderly priest of St. Anne's Catholic Church. He's the one who convinced the Coopers to stay when they returned to visit Mack in the mid-90s. They agreed and opened the Log Cabin Café, which Dolly now owned and operated as the Hut. Rohan and Martía suddenly had to abandon their business and pack up and leave when a certain nosey city inspector came snooping around a few years back, threatening to expose whatever they were hiding.

"We don't want to raise any more suspicions." Martía looked at Dolly knowingly.

The incident with Donovan Huckly, the community's nosey 'Inspector General,' and Tommy Fairbanks, the editor of the *Sugar Pine Station Bulletin*, flashed through Ma's mind. She cringed at the memory.

Fortunately, that episode was behind them, thanks to Martía's 'Forgettable Pie.' The recipe certainly lived up to its name; eating just one piece had erased whatever suspicions the two men had about the Coopers and their connection with the Hut. It was definitely a recipe worth keeping!

Ma had discovered a number of unique and wonderful recipes that her friend had recorded in her willowy handwritten script. They all contained some strange and mysterious spice or ingredient that seemed to unleash a kind of magical result. Dolly thought back to her own experience with the index cards she'd found. The effects of the Memory Cake and those Irresistible Doughnuts certainly bordered on the miraculous. Her reflections brought a smile to her face and led her to consider Mack, who had a hand—*or paw!*—in the discovery of those recipes.

"Speaking of suspicious," Dolly said, her smile weakening, "Mack's long-tenured presence is enough to raise some eyebrows, I imagine."

"Yes, this is true. Especially if you happen to take him to see Doc Moore again."

Dr. Gerald Moore, was the town's veterinarian. A few weeks back, he'd attended to a particular gray tabby, who'd been quite ill. In fact, he had the unfortunate job of pronouncing Mack dead later that very same day. Oi! Would he be surprised to see the cat now!

"I guess we could tell Gerry that we found a replacement kitty?" Ma suggested. Mack, sitting on the counter of an antique-like hutch that loomed over the back room, objected to the possibility with dismissive *meow*.

Martía shrugged. "Very few people want to believe the obvious, so yes, that will likely be enough to sidetrack him. It's when a man becomes solely obsessed with an idea, no matter how irrational it may sound to others, that he will do everything within his power to follow that idea down the path to its final destination."

Dolly blinked and reflected on this as she stuffed a stray strand of hair back into her hairnet. "You know, that is mighty profound for 4:30 in the morning!" Both women laughed and settled into the final thirty minutes of prep time before opening the café.

Their routine was soon interrupted when they heard a tentative knock at the back door.

"Now who could that be?" Ma wondered out loud. Mack answered her musing with a yowl as if he were a king's attendant announcing the next guest at a royal ball. She gave him a sidelong glance as she opened the door.

"Why, Gerry...Doc Moore, we were just..." She waved somewhat airily at Martía. "I mean, come in, come in."

Gerry, his face flushed and with a nervous manner, not at all like his normal calm and steady professional demeanor, entered and shut the door behind him. He looked around and seemed relieved, though when his eyes settled on Mack, they grew wide in surprise.

"Is that...?" He pointed.

Martía quickly volunteered, "He looks like Mack. And, um, we call him Mack. And...oh yes, he arrived the day after the *first* Mack died."

Which was all true enough, as far as the story went.

Continue reading about Ma, Mack, and all the rest of our friends at Sugar Pine Station in the next book, *Ma Tutt's Secret Spice*. Available soon!

## ABOUT THE WRITER

Lyndon Perry teaches secondary level English, is a part-time preacher, full-time husband, and grateful father of two. He enjoys coffee way too much and tries to corral two cats in his spare time. He's more successful at drinking coffee. In addition to preparing lesson plans, Lyndon writes and publishes a variety of speculative fiction. He blogs about writing, reading, and culture at www.lyndonperrywriter.com.

.

Made in the USA
Middletown, DE
24 September 2019